FAIS DO DO DIE

The Big Uneasy Book Five

PAULINE BAIRD JONES

ISBN: 978-1-942583-79-0

❄ Created with Vellum

Fais Do Do Die

He kicks down doors, and she serves *hors d'oeu-vres*. And the Big Uneasy delivers them both a huge helping of high-stakes danger—and a chance at romance.

A happy-ending skeptic and caterer, Sarah Burland, has a high-profile gig at a fundraiser. It's a coup for her catering company until murder kills the party spirit and triggers a hostage situation.

SWAT Team Member Calvin Baker's job cost him his marriage. He's done with romance—even if he does find himself taking an interest in a family friend, Sarah, from time to time. He's sure his feelings are platonic until he finds out she's caught in a hostage situation.

Cal's team affects a rescue, but Sarah's troubles aren't over. The victim's friends—and enemies—keep trouble cooking, and the deeper they dig, the more confusing things get—and the more their attraction to each other grows.

Can the cook and the cop survive long enough to work out their differences? Take a ride into another installment in the engaging Big Uneasy series and find out!

Author's Note

Fais Do Do - (fey doh doh) a country dance party

Chapter One

THE *FAIS DO DO GOOD* was going splendidly—until it wasn't.

Sarah Burland had glanced around with a cautious glow of satisfaction. She never counted her broths until the last drop of gumbo was gone. But so far it looked like a win for Blue Bayou Catering—and that it had raised a lot of money for breast cancer research. The ticket price for the event was sky-high, and the games and prizes were super high end. This group knew how to run an event, one reason Sarah was happy to work for them, even if it put her within snubbing range of her old social circle.

Traffic to and around the buffet table had moved smoothly. The food looked and tasted good, and the ice sculpture, a modern thing of shards and colors, was hanging in there thanks to some weird technology she'd never heard of and some dry ice giving off a drift of fog. The shards floated gracefully in a rainbow-colored pool that had a self-cycling system which made the shards appear to rise and fall. It was, according to the artist, a symbol for breast cancer and healing.

It was also "do not touch." Those shards were sharp, as more than one guest had found out. In the *whatever* column, it was unique and had garnered much praise from the guests—those who hadn't touched it. The artist had offered a different original design as a raffle prize, too. Because who didn't want their own never-melting ice sculpture?

The washboard player, and the rest of the band, might be wearing tuxes—sans ties for safety's sake—but the music was the real *fais do do* deal. The guests had loosened up enough for the spry to start quick-stepping around the dance floor. And on the edges, the alcohol-induced chatter had competed with the music at the height of the party.

Even better, Sarah had managed to be in the kitchen at just the right time to avoid most of her parents' old friends and their sympathetic looks at her "fall from grace."

Sarah had no doubt that her parents were rolling over in their crypt because she'd turned the family home on St. Charles into a catering company. The thing about rolling in crypts? They had doors, not windows, so she couldn't see any rolling, making it not her problem. It wasn't as if her and her parents hadn't diverged on their life views well before their untimely deaths.

She liked cooking, she liked owning her own business, and hard work didn't scare her. She glanced down at her hands. Her manicure—one without polish of course—

didn't stand a chance when she started cooking. She'd picked up a few more cuts and a couple of burns, but that was not unusual. Sarah might be wearing her little black dress, but she was a working chef and proud of it.

"Good evening, Sarah," a voice purred behind her.

A voice with a hint of Russian to it, it was a voice its owner probably considered sexy. With a sigh, Sarah turned to face Dimitri Afoniki, a sexy-in-a-creepy-way crime boss—or so Sarah assumed. It wasn't like she kept up on crime bosses, but he had been the heir apparent to his great uncle, slash wise guy crime boss who died last year.

"I like the red hair," he added, with even more purr.

Sarah had wondered this morning if going red had been a mistake. It was never a good idea to get her hair done when her hormones were doing their monthly rampage. The red had been there before, held back by the blonde, but that day all she could see was red. Not even to herself did Sarah admit she might have done it because all the Baker girls were blonde and it was hard to stand out in a crowd.

Sarah managed a stiff smile because this was business and Afoniki was a guest. She murmured something inde-terminate and eased back a step.

"We never did have that dinner," he murmured, sliding closer.

Sarah eased back some more. She had no intention of having dinner with him, but couldn't help but wonder what she'd do if he got more pushy. How badly did a rejected crime boss act?

"We're both busy people," she said, her smile getting stiffer. Her feeding people, him killing them. She almost frowned. He'd been at a lot of these charity dos recently. Was he trying to clean up his public image?

He was a handsome man—if one liked stalking, blond tigers with sharply chiseled features and cold eyes. She didn't. With his gaze on her—she could almost sense his tail switching from side to side—she didn't let her thoughts stray to the kind of man she did like. Not with Afoniki's gaze trying to dissect her thoughts.

"I'd clear my schedule for you," he half growled, half purred, shifting so that they were closer once more.

She blinked, fighting the urge to roll her eyes at him. Did lines like that really work? His heavy cologne tickled her nose and she wondered what he'd do if she sneezed on him.

It wasn't naive to wonder what game he was playing. He stalked in and out of her life at random intervals, leading her to the perfectly logical conclusion that she wasn't who he was really interested in. Or that he got bored with the yes-women too lazy to look further than his pretty face. It could be that simple—and that annoying. She didn't have time to play games with a dangerous creep.

"Sarah," the gentle, fluting voice managed to be heard over the music and the chatting. Afoniki's gaze flashed briefly with annoyance.

No surprise gentle old ladies weren't his thing. With a look that tried to be apologetic—and probably failed— Sarah turned her attention and her body toward Miss

Maisie Daigle who was—in this world—far more important than a rather minor crime figure.

Miss Maisie had been a fixture in New Orleans
society for as long as Sarah could recall. She was one of
those pink-and-white old ladies that younger women tried
to scorn but wilted and faded away when they encoun-
tered her gentle ruthless gaze. The wealthy widow of
Roger Daigle, parties and fundraisers failed if she wasn't
there. But, unlike many with that kind of financial power,
Maisie was nice. Not so nice that people rolled over her,
but universally liked by people with sense and respected
by the people who wanted to matter.

She had to be in her nineties, Sarah thought, or close
to. She had a halo of white around her crumpled paper
face. Her eyes were a pale blue and the wrinkled bow of
her mouth curved up, even as she gave Afoniki a
measuring gaze that caused him to retreat.

Now that was a superpower Sarah could wish for. She
resisted the urge to high five Maisie. She wasn't a high-
fiving kind of old lady. And it might break her.

"Thanks," Sarah said, settling for a grin that lit an
amused twinkle in the faded gaze. Maisie's clothes were
nice, but not obscenely expensive, and the large bag over
a bent arm reminded Sarah of Miss Marple—or at least
how she imagined the fictional sleuth might look. There
were, as the saying went, no flies on Maisie. She was
surprised the old lady could stand upright with the huge
bag hanging off her arm. She looked like a gentle breeze
would knock her over, but like most Southern women,
Maisie was iron on the inside.

"I don't think he's a nice man," she murmured.

This was the worst Maisie was known to say about anyone.

"No, he's not," Sarah agreed with more force than tact.

The pale gaze settled on Sarah's face. "Is he bothering you?"

Sarah hesitated. "I think he likes…bothering people when he's bored. It never lasts."

"Women. He bothers women," Maisie said. She gave a tiny sniff that said more than words.

"I think he bothers men when he feels like it," Sarah said, thinking about Nell's husband, Alex. Nell was her best friend and Alex was a cop and a Baker—one of seven sons with six sisters—the blonde crowd she'd maybe hoped to stand out in. It must be tough for him when Nell was related to two local crime families. Afoniki belonged to a third, which made things…interesting. Was that why he hung around? Trying to keep tabs on the other families? Sarah hadn't seen the other two titular heads of those families tonight, but that didn't mean they weren't here.

Even if she'd wanted a date with the creep—which she didn't—with Nell and Alex renting Sarah's third floor, she had no desire to stir the Baker pot that much. She did know her pots and stirring.

"He's trouble like his great uncle," Miss Maisie said. Her lips pursed briefly in distaste.

"You knew Alexsi?" Sarah shouldn't be surprised.

Miss Maisie's knowledge of the city and its people was as deep and wide as the Mississippi river.

"Well, knew of," she admitted. She eased closer to Sarah and lowered her voice, the hand not being pulled down by the handbag resting on Sarah's arm. "Might have met him once or twice. Back in the day he was more handsome than that rascal of a nephew."

Sarah felt her eyes widen.

"But I always know." Maisie's grip tightened on Sarah's arm with surprising force. Apparently the inner iron extended to the outside. "I've always known," Miss Maisie murmured, her gaze getting that distant look that the elderly got when the past enveloped them

"Known…what?" Sarah prompted, her voice soft.

"Who was good. And who wasn't." Miss Maisie's gaze suddenly focused and her hand dropped free of Sarah's. "It's kept me mostly out of trouble."

Sarah opened her mouth, then closed it again and grinned. Bet the "mostly" was a good story. But that was another of the nice things about Maisie. She didn't gossip. Or spend too much time "remembering when."

Miss Maisie shifted, so that she could see Afoniki, talking to an animated young debutante, his face lit with charm. "There's trouble coming with that one, you mark my words."

Sarah nodded, hoping the trouble wouldn't touch her or Nell. She didn't have time for trouble.

But, of course it did.

CALVIN BAKER'S dad was a master of wordless disapproval. It emanated in all directions from Zach's usual place at the head of the battered Baker kitchen table. It was ironic, but also no use pointing this out, because Zach had never once said he didn't approve of his son's choice to train for New Orleans' equivalent of SWAT. Cal's ex-wife had been more vocal with her disapproval. He'd heard it said that if the Marines were supposed to have wives, they'd have been issued one. The same could be said for being in a police tactical squad.

If Zach could have divorced him, it was possible he would have—hence the irony, since Zach was a retired cop. But in Zach's day, he'd been known to assert, there'd been no SWAT nonsense—which wasn't exactly true. Special Weapons and Tactical groups dated back to the 1960s. But Zach was a beat cop who'd worked his way up to detective. And that's how his sons were supposed to do it.

Zach hadn't been thrilled about Cal's time in the Organized Crime Unit. And then Cal had been invited—and accepted that invite—for an assignment in SWAT. And because they were Bakers, Cal didn't know how to explain to his dad that, while he'd also been born with "serve and protect" in his DNA, he'd been bored by his time on the regular beat. If he'd tried, Zach would have pointed out that when Cal wasn't kicking down doors, he was driving a beat in the worst parts of the city. His choice was not without irony.

It was the crap beat his ex hated even more than the door-kicking. There was no question it had gotten increasingly dangerous to be a cop—let alone one patrolling the projects. He'd been shot one too many times. It wasn't as if he liked being shot, he'd protested, but it had already been too late. The thread that held them together had snapped long before the shooting. He just hadn't realized it. She'd waited until he was out of the hospital to leave. He'd told her not to bother, but she'd always cared what people thought.

Cal didn't miss her, a fact that bothered him because he'd planned to stay married for life, like Zach who had married and buried two wives. Loyalty was also imprinted on the Baker DNA. He did miss living with a woman. Even a serially annoyed woman softened the edges of a man's world, left their soft scent lingering in the air after they passed. He'd take the fights over going home to silence and furred food in the fridge.

But he'd never again assume that a woman could handle his job when his own tough-as-boots dad couldn't.

He looked up and caught a sympathetic look from his dad's—he made himself think it—girlfriend, Becca Poole. She offered him a second helping of dessert in lieu of comment. He took the bread pudding and scooped up another spoonful, even though he was full—also in lieu of comment.

"It's good, thanks," he said, breaking the silence with an effort. He managed to not look at his watch. It wouldn't move any faster than the kitchen clock over his dad's shoulder.

He glanced around, noting that Becca had begun to soften Zach's home. A touch here and there. Was she

afraid they'd object to her replacing the hammered furni-
ture of their youth? With thirteen kids from Zach's two
marriages, the place had taken a beating. Maybe she'd up
her efforts after the wedding. She hadn't moved in, as far
as any of them could tell. And truth be told, none of
them wanted to know if she had. It was in the realm of
things you didn't want to know about your dad, not to
mention embarrassing that his dad had a more active
dating life than Cal did.

"Thank you." Becca's cheeks flushed and she bit her
lip, probably trying to think of a noncontroversial conversation topic.

The trouble with Zach was, any topic could turn into
a minefield if you weren't up on the family gossip. Cal
was only up on the latest egress techniques.

With a quick, sidelong look at Zach, Becca took a dive
into deep waters.

"Ben says you're working on a robotics project."

Cal nodded, also giving his dad a quick glance. "We
don't have the budget for anything fancy, but I like
tinkering."

Zach made a sound that could have been a snort. Or
a cough.

"Do you program it yourself?" Becca persisted.

Was she really interested, or fed up with the silence?
Cal couldn't tell.

"I program, too," he admitted. He'd always been
interested, but it had languished until his divorce, freeing
up large chunks of time. He'd enjoyed strategy computer
games until he joined SWAT. After he'd done the real

thing, the games never quite measured up, though he still kept his hand in with a few of his favorites. He liked figuring out how to win.

Cal pushed his plate away and leaned back. He still had about ten minutes before he could leave without too many glares.

"Anything interesting happening?" Cal asked into the silence. He looked at Zach, then at Becca.

The edges of Becca's mouth quivered. Good thing she had a sense of humor.

"I think everyone is okay?" she said, making it a question as she once again looked at Zach, her expression hitting somewhere between reproving and amused. She half moved a hand, as if she wanted to cover Zach's with hers, and stopped herself.

They all must be fun to be around. Cal found it easy to give her a real smile.

"Alex and Nell went to Mississippi," Zach said, his expression softening. He covered her hand with his with no sign of embarrassment.

Cal tried to recall if he'd ever seen his dad embarrassed. Probably hadn't ever had time.

"Some beach time, they said," Becca added. "Didn't Ben have a date tonight?"

Cal found his stomach tightening for no good reason. It wasn't as if his brother's dating life was his business.

"Sarah?" Cal asked, his tone carefully indifferent.

"No," Becca said, shaking her head. "Sarah's working tonight. A charity do in the warehouse district, I believe."

Cal didn't shift under her innocent, but somehow

intent gaze. Thought he hid an inappropriate relief, too. Good thing his dad hadn't met her when Cal was a teenager. He had a feeling not much got by her. It wasn't like he had time—was interested in Sarah. He was just curious which brother, Frank or Ben, would win the lady. She was, as Frank put it, a cool drink of water—who was very good at hiding what she thought and which brother she preferred. Nell said it was all those years with massively embarrassing parents. Cal knew about embarrassing parents.

"Ingrid's on duty tonight," Zach said. He shot Cal a look under his brows. "Like you."

Not quite like Cal, but he didn't point out that his sister was a crime scene investigator who showed up after the bullets quit flying. Zach knew it, but still wasn't thrilled about his little girl's line of work either.

"I'll probably run into her then," Cal said, meeting the look calmly. If he'd been a beat cop, he would have, too. The murder rate had improved the last year, but shootings hadn't gone down much. And odds were high where he patrolled. Even the people who lived there didn't like being there at night. Situationally, he shouldn't like it either, but he didn't mind night shifts.

The silence built again. Cal presumed the rest of his siblings were fine, or at least hadn't done anything to annoy their dad. Jillian had once suggested they use an online spreadsheet to keep everyone updated on who was where. Though it was a semi-joke in the city, none of the Baker kids really liked "baking"—more than one of the Bakers showing up at—a crime scene.

It might be another reason he'd opted for SWAT. He'd heard jokes about family reunions at crime scenes. It wasn't easy to carve out a unique place for yourself when you were one of thirteen.

With relief, he saw that pumpkin time had arrived. He could leave the party. He pushed his chair back and did the polite. Becca held his hand for a moment longer than usual, and to his surprise, he found himself pecking her cheek. She looked surprised, too, but also happy. Must be tough for her to crack a family as dense and laconic as theirs.

Zach made a half move to give him a hug. Cal completed the move, wrapping his arms around his dad, surprised as always that he—who had always seemed larger-than-life—was actually shorter. As hard as it was, because he was his father's son, he always hugged his family goodbye when he was with one of them. He knew that every time he left, it could be the last time.

Chapter Two

THE PARTY WAS WINDING DOWN, the guests starting to thin out, leaving the one Sarah called "well lit." It sounded less judge-y than "drunk." The kind of toney crowd attracted to fundraisers didn't like to smudge their images by getting too drunk—but it was late and the press had already left. Sarah and her crew were discreetly cleaning up by gradually reducing the buffet length. She noted that the ice sculpture was performing as advertised. That "crete" stuff, cryo…create?—was amazing. She tipped her head to one side. Was it a bit off balance? She shrugged. Not her problem.

She heard a high-pitched giggle and turned to look at the dance floor. The giggle appeared to have come from Afoniki's dance partner. He was dancing with the debutante he'd been schmoozing earlier. His four bodyguards, sober and cold-eyed, were positioned protectively against the walls.

Off to one side, Miss Maisie was sedately shifting

slightly from side to side with her escort, Valentin Laurent. The old guy was as much a legend as Miss Maisie, though for different reasons. He'd been, well, an escort, before it was popular. Even Sarah's mom had been less scornful about him, though that was probably because Miss Maisie looked out for him. But, according to those who'd know, he'd been something in his day. Handsome, discreet, lots of stamina—he had everything but the money to match his style. Sarah's gaze followed the couple for a few seconds, her mind spinning a bit about what stories he could tell, though they'd probably go with him to his grave.

The music had slowed as the witching hour approached. For Sarah, she and her feet had at least another hour before they were done. Her feet knew it and weren't happy about it. She surreptitiously moved her shoulders to ease the cramp and glanced at her watch. Technically this do was done—

She heard another giggle, one with a coy protest in it, and returned her attention to Afoniki and his deb. She'd pulled back in mock protest. As Sarah watched, Afoniki tugged her closer, his mouth smiling but his eyes bored. With a flirtatious smile, the deb allowed herself to be pulled into his arms, the girl's arms sliding around to his back. It kind of creeped Sarah out, but before she could look away, the deb let out a startled cry, yanking away from the bad guy.

The deb's hands were stretched out in front, her horrified gaze going from the something dark smeared across her hands and then back to Afoniki. He swayed, his gaze startled, perhaps puzzled, but then slowly going unfocused.

Sarah blinked. *What the—*

The deb's scream was choked, almost a shrill gasp.

Against the walls, his bodyguards had stiffened to heightened attention. Confusion turned the nearby dancers into milling, confused bystanders, and then some realization not apparent to Sarah began to flow over them. Hands went to mouths. Sounds of distress began to build. The deb backed away from him like the distressed heroine from a melodrama, joined by others who faded back, leaving Afoniki swaying alone in the center of the dance floor.

His bodyguards surged forward. One of them caught him as he stumbled forward, and it was only then that Sarah saw something sticking out of Afoniki's back.

The bodyguard held up a hand that was smeared red. *Blood.*

The deb and some of the other women loosed low moans that began to rise to screams.

The other three bodyguards suddenly all held weapons as the music faltered to a stop. So did the screams as everyone stared at the guns.

"No one move," one of them snarled into the sudden silence.

Just when things were going so smoothly toward a tidy departure.

SARAH WAS INSIDE.

Cal stood silently with his squad, his body relaxed on the outside, his insides churning. Around him milled street cops, reporters, a couple of ambulances, the inevitable onlookers, and a Lucky Dog truck. Lights tracked across a scene with tepid help from the streetlights. Out on the river, a ship's horn blew sadly.

One fatality.

The shaken girl, in a Blue Bayou Catering uniform, wasn't sure who had died, just that someone had. She was the only one who'd seen anything and she hadn't seen much.

"One of the guests, I think," she'd added. "Miss Burland, our boss, signaled for us to run, so we did." She explained—again—that Sarah had released the wait staff when things started to wind down. Only the kitchen and cleanup staff were still on duty.

"How many people in the main room?"

"Maybe thirty? There was the band—six people, maybe, the bartender and he might have one of his waiters left. Guests? Twenty to twenty-five. Could be more. Could be less. Party was almost over."

"Did you see weapons? Guns?"

She thought she remembered one, maybe more. She wasn't sure.

"When did you realize something was wrong?"

They were cleaning up what they could, loading the truck. She heard shouts and then the music stopped in the middle of a song. She'd looked out the kitchen door and that's when she saw her boss signal her to get out.

"What did you do next?"

"We argued for maybe a minute, but someone screamed in the other room. We ran out and hid behind the truck. Called nine-one-one. And then hid inside the truck and locked the doors."

"You have no idea how many assailants there are?"

"No."

"Any idea what started it?"

"No."

"Any names of people left inside, other than Miss Burland?"

"No. There was a reporter there earlier. She might know."

Only if she wasn't still inside, Cal thought.

"Any idea where we can get a contact number for the organizer."

"The paperwork might be in the truck."

Someone left to check on that. Someone else was working on getting a building layout plan. It was harder in the middle of the night. They'd have to wake someone up and sometimes they had to go somewhere else to get the information.

And all the while the clock ticked, an unanswered question for each tick and tock.

"We're trying to get a line inside, to open a dialogue with someone in there," the official spokesman for the NOPD was telling a growing cadre of reporters.

A negotiator was incoming, according to Big Chip, their squad commander. They were trying to get a guest list so they could try some cell numbers.

Cal cleared his throat. "I might know a number."
Sarah's had showed up on group texts from his siblings.
He'd saved it, he didn't know why, he just had. He pulled
it up and sent it to Big Chip. He got an iron-eyed look in
response.

"You gonna be okay if we go in, Ghost?"

If? Big Chip wasn't usually an optimist. Cal gave a
short, sharp nod.

The chaos swirled around him. Normally he didn't
notice, his thoughts totally focused on his part of the job.
But it had never been this personal. Alex and Nell were
out of town. If anything happened to Sarah on his
watch—

Words penetrated the swirl.

"No answer on that number you gave me."

"Her cell is probably still in the kitchen," the kitchen
staff girl said and added something about spam calls.

"We need eyes inside," BuzzKill said. He'd earned the
call sign by killing a lot of buzz.

Cal's chin came up. He exchanged a glance with
Eclipse. It was a sore point that the department couldn't
afford to get them all the cool toys, so they filled in where
they could, especially the ones, like Cal, who weren't
trying to support a family on cop pay.

"It's worth a try," he said.

"Commander," Cal said, moving closer to the
commander. "I've got my robot here." He'd taken to
bringing it along. Just in case. And he'd earned his call
sign for being a ghost when one was needed.

Big Chip stared at him, then turned and looked at the

facade of the reclaimed warehouse. It was lit up like a circus.

"We've got some guys looking for roof access," the commander said, almost absently.

From what they could tell from witness statements, it was a long way down to the dance floor.

"We could go in the back, through the kitchen, same way the staff exited," Cal said, keeping his tone and gaze noncommittal. The first on-scene cops had checked. The suspects hadn't locked down that outside door.

The commander nodded reluctantly. "Talk to the kitchen staff. You need to know if there is anything to watch out for. Take BuzzKill, FunSize and Pluto with you. And don't shoot unless—"

"I know the rules of engagement," Cal said, still no change in his tone.

———

ONE OF AFONIKI'S bodyguards stood over the body. The other three paced restlessly around the hostages. Hostages and one murderer, Sarah reminded herself.

It had to have been someone in this room.

The goons had figured that out, but they didn't know what to do about it, Sarah decided. So they'd herded everyone over to the stage. Sitting on the hard floor was not fun, but the real torture was trying to keep her hands clasped behind her neck. She glanced at Miss Maisie and Valentin. If it was hard on her, it must be killer on the two oldsters. Miss Maisie caught her look and gave her a tired smile. Valentin gave her a slow nod that somehow managed to be stately.

Because of the position of her hands, she couldn't see her watch, but it felt like they'd been sitting there for hours. So probably not more than an hour? Or less. Had her staff gotten clear? It still shocked her that none of the goons had checked the kitchen. It was as if it didn't exist to them.

They'd found the only charity person left, the one with the keys, and locked the front doors. She'd heard that goon tell the others that there were cops outside.

Why had they lost their heads and taken hostages? What would make a goon afraid? Failure? Was there someone behind Afoniki who would punish them? She found that a little hard to believe. Not that she knew a lot about crime families, but on television, there was always someone waiting in the wings for any sign of weakness so they could take over. And they'd probably reward anyone who made it possible.

Of course, that takeover usually resulted in collateral damage for those around the old "king."

Even factoring in that scenario, taking hostages still didn't seem like a good plan. And it looked like they were starting to figure that out—if the low-voiced arguing was any indication.

She didn't want them, or anyone here to become collateral damage, too.

At one point she'd heard her phone ringing faintly in the kitchen, her it's-probably-a-spam-call ringtone. The goons had tensed, conferred briefly, but no one had gone to answer it. They hadn't even gone and checked out the kitchen. Didn't they have kitchens in the mad, bad world of crime?

She should be grateful they'd missed an entry point, but it was hard to be grateful for anything with her tush signaling it had had enough.

She tried to shift, and one of the goons swung his attention—and his weapon—her way.

She gave him what she hoped was a wan and defeated look.

"This is really uncomfortable," she said. "Can we at least put our arms down?"

He stared at her for a long hard moment.

"You searched everyone," she pointed out. "We're no threat to you." She was aware of the irony of her words. One of them had killed a top mob boss with a shard from that ice sculpture, apparently in front of everyone in the room. But she hoped irony was not a goon's strong suit.

Finally, he nodded. The wave of relieved sighs must have washed over him, but it might have felt good. The room was still stuffy from all the bodies that had crowded in here earlier.

Now that she could see her watch, she almost wished she couldn't. It had been a long day, an endless night, and now a crappy beginning to a new day.

Sarah wasn't sure why, perhaps there was sympathy along with the tired in her eyes, but for whatever reason, the one who seemed to be in charge of the goons approached her. He lowered his gun and held out a hand to her. After a short hesitation, Sarah took it. At least it would get her off her butt.

He released her hand as soon as she was up.

"Come." Like his ex-boss, he had a distinct Russian accent.

Sarah arched the crick out of her back and then followed him, wincing. Her butt wasn't quite ready for walking. And she wasn't eager to be led over to the body.

Afoniki, in death, his face slack, had lost what charm he'd had. Even the evil was gone. He was just a body.

He'd slumped half on his side when he went down and no one had moved him, which left the hole in his back visible. Blood had trickled out onto the stone floor, though not as much as she'd have expected—based on her wide experience with British crime shows. Maybe the ice shard had slowed the bleeding?

Some of it remained but there were signs of the water from it diluting some of the blood on the floor.

"Killer in this room," the goon said.

Sarah couldn't argue with that, so she didn't. She looked up and met a gaze that still had all of its evil intact.

"Yes." She hesitated, biting her lip, trying to organize thoughts with an exhausted brain. "You need to let the police in to investigate. We could be damaging crime scene evidence."

A measure of contempt entered his gaze. "You know this how?"

She half shrugged. "I watch…television."

This did not seem to bother him, because he nodded.

"Is—" he used a Russian word that she suspected had a counterpart in English that started with an "f."

She nodded again. "It can be fixed. No one has...no one else has died. You didn't do this." She gestured toward the body. "You got upset—understandably upset and things got a little...weird."

"Police won't understand...weird." For a moment he almost looked amused. Human.

She half smiled. "I'll bet they understand it better than you think." She hesitated. "This is New Orleans."

He laughed then and the transformation was amazing. It was probably the face his mother saw. His wife, if he had one.

"How do we fix...weird?"

Sarah let her breath ease out in a quiet sigh and glanced toward the kitchen.

And saw a piece of something sticking out from under the door.

CAL WENT IN FIRST, his team stacked behind him. He was the ghost on the team. BuzzKill came in on his six, going left as Cal went right.

Food was still scattered across some of the counters, open containers waiting for filling. He saw a purse and ghosted over to it. Sarah's. He recognized it, which might be sad.

He felt the slight shift of air as the rest of the team joined him. He signaled toward the door and they moved that way, his team taking up protective positions as he knelt to get out his flexible camera. A pity the door didn't have windows in it, but it was what it was.

He slid the filament through the gap between the door and the floor and then pulled out the tablet, and tried to figure out what the camera sent him. He tinkered with the settings and suddenly he could see.

It took him a moment to find Sarah—her hair seemed darker than usual, but that was her, no question— standing in a semicircle with four armed men, though their handguns hung loosely down at their sides. A body lay on the floor close to where they stood. Off to the right, a group that he figured were hostages, sat on the floor.

He turned his attention back to the targets and saw Sarah's attention turn their way. He froze. She didn't. With a slow motion, she lifted a hand to brush her hair back, using the movement to turn her head back to the man in front of her.

He turned up the sound playing through one of his earbuds.

"Let's figure out how to get you out of this," she said, easily, despite the tension visible in the line of her back.

"This would be...good," the man admitted.

Russian? Cal blinked. He wished he could get a better look at the body, but this wasn't the time.

"I know this probably goes against the grain and your training, but what if"—she hesitated and took a deep breath, one visible from where Cal crouched—"you put your weapons on the floor and we could all kneel and, you know"—she gestured vaguely—"put our hands behind our necks."

There was a pause. "You said you were tired," the perp pointed out.

Cal found he could almost grin.

"I'm so tired, you have no idea," Sarah admitted. "It's been a really long day and even when this is over, it's not over for me."

"Or for me," the man admitted. Again, he hesitated. "How will they"— he made a gesture toward the outside —"know we are unarmed?"

"Well, that is a problem for sure," she admitted, licking lips that were probably dry, "but on television, the guys, the SWAT guys, have eyes on, well, your guys by now." She tried a smile that wasn't half bad. "I really don't want to get shot, even though access to pain meds is kind of appealing right now because I am that tired, which assumes the shots don't kill me. Not ready to die."

The guy stared at her for what felt like a long time, then he smiled. "Nor am I."

He looked at the other three guys and said something in Russian. They all glanced around, though none of them looked in the direction that was a problem for them, Cal noted.

"Get ready," Cal told his team. His commander tried to cut in to request a status update, but Cal cut him off. "Not now."

The four Russians—this would probably matter to him later—slowly extended their arms, as if the cops were already inside with guns on them, then lowered their guns to the floor. They backed up the required distance and knelt, carefully lifting their arms and putting their hands on the backs of their heads.

Sarah, without looking in his direction, eased herself down—it looked like it hurt and Cal's adrenalin spiked—then she also clasped her hands behind her neck.

"We can go in," Cal said as he rose smoothly to his feet.

Chapter Three

BY THE TIME Cal got back outside, the scene had been "baked." Ingrid was there as part of the Crime Scene unit, and Ben—he didn't know why his gut tightened at the sight of his big brother—was there in his role of homicide detective. Ben didn't see him right away. He exited the car and headed inside to his—now—crime scene.

As Cal stripped off his SWAT gear, handed in his weapons, and went through the post-incident assessment, he covertly studied Sarah.

Only she, the bartender, and the members of the band had been allowed outside. None of them had been in any position to commit the murder. The rest were suspects in the death of Dimitri Afoniki. A bunch of half-drunk society types, and an old lady, an old man. There was a perp walk for you. Tonight he was glad he wasn't Ben.

Sarah sat on the back of an ambulance sipping a bottle of water. She looked tired, but still—his thoughts hesitated before settling on—good. She looked good, though her hair still puzzled him. He thought it was lighter, blonder, though he liked the red. But she was alive. It could have gone wrong so many ways and it hadn't.

There was still a bit of a tremor in his hands from the adrenaline. And he was relieved he didn't have to tell Alex and Nell that Sarah…his thoughts choked. Well, she was all right. The crime team had decided not to make the kitchen part of their crime scene when Sarah offered them the remaining food. Nicely played. They'd let her staff in to clear the serving dishes and such. Everything in the main room was part of the crime scene. The last of her staff handed her the truck keys and then headed toward a waiting Uber ride. Her shoulders drooped and she rubbed her eyes with her free hand. Cal hesitated, then crossed over to her.

"I could drive you home," he said. Ben wouldn't be done for hours.

Sarah looked up, her smile tired. "Am I allowed to leave?"

"Ben knows where you live," he said, half jesting, half…something.

Her lashes flicked down and her mouth straightened. "That he does," she said lightly and pushed herself up.

This brought her closer to Cal than he was expecting. She swayed slightly and his hands shot out, gripping her upper arms to steady her. She looked up and smiled.

"Thanks. I think I'm done," her gaze moved to her truck. "And still work to do."

"Be glad to help," Cal said, his voice unexpectedly husky.

She looked up again. In the lamp and emergency lighting, her eyes were smudged with tired, but still warm with gratitude. She was grateful, that was all. That was enough, he reminded himself. He wasn't going to get into a fight with his brothers—the curve of her lips and the warmth, the smell of woman wrapped around him. He'd forgotten...

"Cal!" The sound of Ben's voice made her jerk. "Sarah!"

For a moment, it almost seemed as if annoyance flashed in Sarah's eyes, but her lashes slid down.

Ben jogged over, his gaze moving between them. Cal realized he still held her by the forearms, but he wasn't sure she could stand on her own. Sarah turned, and his hands fell to his sides. There was a chill from the loss of contact swept through him. It made no sense on the hot summer night.

"You all right?" Ben's gaze scanned her.

"I'm fine, other than tired and sore—from sitting on the hard floor for so long," she said as concern flashed on Ben's face. "Cal's going to drive me home."

"I'll get your statement tomorrow," Ben said, his gaze shifting to Cal. "Thanks, little brother."

Cal fought the stab of annoyance and nodded. Ben seemed to hesitate as his attention turned back to Sarah, but she was already turning away, a tired, "'Night, Ben," offered over her shoulder.

Cal fell in next to her, matching his stride to her shorter one. You'd think a guy with six sisters would know how to talk to girls, but the genes from their dad were strong—though he'd managed to talk three women into marrying him—if he got Becca to the altar. Of course, if his sisters were right, Becca was having issues with what she called "wrinkly romance."

He moved ahead of her to unlock the passenger door and hovered until she'd pulled herself up onto the seat. She was fumbling with the seat belt when he closed the door and trotted around to the driver's side. Inside the van, the smell of food—good food—lingered, reminding him that he was hungry. Maybe he could score some supper even if he couldn't...he shut the thought off.

"It's so ironic," Sarah broke the silence. "I've been around food all night and didn't get any. I'm so hungry. Good thing I have food at home."

Cal's relief at the thought of food loosened his smile as he reached to insert the keys in the ignition.

"You should do that more often," Sarah said.

"Do what?" Cal fired the ignition.

"Smile. You have a great smile."

He was too badass to blush, so that wasn't heat he felt in his face as he put the truck in gear.

"It sticks a little when you try for second," she said.

He glanced at her as he fought with second gear. "You do, too. Have a...nice smile, I mean."

"Why, thank you."

CAL DIDN'T SAY much as they unloaded containers from the truck. Now that she thought about it, she'd never heard Cal say much. She didn't say much because she was tired. When they'd stowed what absolutely had to be stowed, Sarah shifted gears to getting them both some food on a plate. The only question she asked him was what he wanted to drink. It was not a shock he picked water. None of the Baker boys or girls drank alcohol. It was a bit unusual until you learned that one of Zach's wives—and mother to the girls—had died because of a drunk driver.

Cal scooped the food into his mouth like he'd been starving. Sarah took it slower so she could watch Cal. She might have wondered if he took time to taste anything, but in the silence, she heard small sounds of satisfaction. If she hadn't been so exhausted, these sounds might have been unsettling. They did help with the post-traumatic chill as shock faded to be replaced with all the might-have-beens.

Cal looked up, his hand freezing halfway to his mouth. His gaze narrowed. "You okay?"

She started to shake her head and decided that was too Baker of her. "I'm starting to realize all the things that could have gone wrong."

"You kept your cool when it mattered. If you want to go to pieces now, you've earned it."

Sarah felt her mouth turn up in a smile. Amazing it had found some energy somewhere. "Thanks. Part of me wants to wail like a baby, but I'm too tired." At these words, tears did prick the corners of her eyes. "I was sure glad to see you and your team."

"The perps had already given up," Cal pointed out.

Sarah met his gaze then. "Not completely. It wouldn't have taken much to shift things the other direction. They were pretty freaked out."

Sarah found her hands clutching the side of her countertop as she remembered staring into the main goon's eyes. Trying to stay calm, as a tic worked at the side of his right eye. And the one who'd studied her like she was a piece of meat.

"They weren't nice men," she murmured, a tremor in her voice she hadn't planned on, as she echoed Maisie's understated assessment.

"No." Cal's hand reached easily across the counter and covered her hand.

Did it feel cold to him? Because heat flowed from his, easing the chill that memory had returned to her body. He had nice eyes, a strong face, and firm mouth. It was easy—or lazy—to think they all looked alike, but they didn't and they weren't. Oh, they were all good guys. Frank was mercurial and amusing. Ben was easygoing with a quiet sense of humor. Sarah wasn't sure what or who Cal was, but she realized she'd like to know.

Seeing him come through that door at the event, his body lethal and graceful had both thrilled and scared her. What they all, or most of the Bakers, did was dangerous, but what Cal did took it up a big notch. She knew through Nell that their dad wasn't thrilled with Cal's choice, but tonight she was grateful for it.

"Thank you," she said, "for saving my—our lives."

He shifted uncomfortably. That was pure Baker boy. But he didn't lift his hand from hers.

"When does Nell get back?" he asked.

"Um" —it took Sarah a minute to make the switch— "not until Sunday night. They've earned the time away," she added when he frowned.

"Maybe we should see if you can stay with…" he paused to consider, "Becca or one of my sisters. Post-traumatic stress is, well, you could have a rough night."

It didn't seem possible with her level of tired.

Sarah looked at her watch. "It's four a.m."

He considered this. "I could sleep on your couch."

The warmth amped up. "I do have guest rooms with actual beds. More than I need, in fact." She saw him hesitate and went on talking to give him time to think—and find an excuse if he needed one. "When my parents died, I thought about going the B&B route, but I'm not cheerful in the morning and I think that's a prerequisite, isn't it? Not growling at the guests to leave you alone. At least it made it easy for Alex and Nell to take over a floor. We're adding in a kitchen up there, you know, for privacy for them—though Nell keeps saying it's not necessary, but they need their space." And it meant she wasn't alone again. She'd almost forgotten how to do alone.

As if he heard the thought, Cal said, "You shouldn't be alone tonight."

He was right, more than he knew. Exhaustion dragged at her, but she didn't want to leave this room, didn't want to leave him and go upstairs alone. Oh, she wasn't thinking about jumping his bones or anything as weird as that. But she'd have liked him to hold her hand all night. She had to make herself pull back when he rose. Big and broad and tough.

When she stood in a thicket of the Baker boys, she'd assumed they'd be smaller separately, but Cal still cast a big shadow. A comforting shadow.

"I would…be glad of the company," she admitted. "What if we both took a couch in the parlor."

"You have two couches?"

"My parents had a lot of couches, so yeah, I have them now."

He blinked, then nodded. "Okay."

IN THE BATHROOM Sarah directed Cal to, he found a new toothbrush and toothpaste—guest sized—mouthwash, soap that wouldn't make him smell like a girl, and fresh towels.

"Alex might have some pajamas you can borrow," she'd also suggested.

Yeah, Alex wore pj's. And pigs flew. Cal did find some jogging sweats that were actually clean and pulled those on. When he came back downstairs, he found Sarah by following the light spilling out into the entrance hall. The first time he'd come here, he'd been a little intimidated maybe. It was St. Charles, a mansion no less. Neither Nell nor Sarah seemed to notice all the antique fittings and fixtures and crap. It was their home and Sarah's business.

But tonight—no, this morning, he reminded himself —this morning it was big and full of shadows. No, she couldn't have stayed alone in this place. He wasn't sure why he felt the need to justify his presence. He wasn't poaching on his brother's territory. He was keeping an eye on her. Ben was working, was probably still working the scene.

For the first time, he wondered who had killed Afoniki. That was a weird location for a hit. He hadn't wasted time studying the body, since it wasn't his problem, but he had noticed there wasn't a visible murder weapon.

He walked into the parlor and caught his breath. Sarah had exchanged her work pants and shirt for a pair of pajamas. They were soft and well washed, and hinted at the body underneath in ways not good for a guy looking out for his brother's girl.

After a small hesitation, he kept going, stopping when he saw the second couch, the one she wasn't sitting on. There was a coffee table between the two couches, but the distance felt too far—and not far enough. The couch was also comfortable, something he hadn't expected based on the antiques in the other rooms on this floor. But it was, he realized, a family-friendly space, their space—Sarah's and Nell's. The couches were worn and comfy, the tables beat-up looking, and there were books and magazines scattered around. A normal-sized television was pushed off to the side, so television could be watched here but wasn't watched that often. There was even a pair of Alex's shoes kicked to one side.

She'd brought in a couple of pillows and blankets. She was an optimist if she thought it would get cold enough for blankets.

Her smile was a bit relieved, he realized, and he wondered if the silence of the old house had unnerved her a bit or if PTSD was kicking in now that shock had had time to wear off.

He bent to arrange his pillow and blanket, not looking at her as he said, "Our minds tend to replay stuff with all the variations for what didn't happen, but could have. Something about short-term memory and shock. You'll probably have nightmares. Best way to deal with them is to find two spots on the ceiling and look at one for twenty-five seconds, then at the other. It helps clear the nightmare so you don't fall back into it when you go back to sleep."

He allowed himself to look then, saw exhaustion, but it didn't take the edge off great. She managed a smile that squeezed his heart some.

"Thanks." She adjusted her pillow and pulled the blanket around her like she was cold. "Oh, the light."

"You should leave it on, so you won't wake up in the dark."

"Right. Good idea." Her hands clenched the blanket, turning the knuckles white.

Now he found himself wondering if she knew

anything that might put her in danger. A mob boss got knocked off at a party she was at. Someone might be unhappy about that, though he couldn't imagine who. He wasn't a detective, but it might be need-to-know.

"Did you see anything?" he asked, wanting to shake his head at the question. It was too vague.

"You mean see who killed him?" She didn't act upset. "I really didn't. I was focused on the table and how long it would be before we could go." She frowned, staring into the distance. "I've been trying to remember because his goons, his guys I mean—"

"Goons is fine," Cal said with a grin.

She chuckled. "They were so shaken up, and yes, scared. It's not a good look on guys that are, well, creepy tough. I remember that more than anything else, because I wasn't sure what they'd do…"

Cal frowned. "What do you mean?"

"Well, the murderer was there, at least, I don't think there was time for anyone to leave, and it would be so obvious, and I didn't notice anyone heading for the exit." Her gaze narrowed, as if this would help her see. "Though I'm not sure I would have. I was looking that way, no, I had been," she said, as if surprised to realize it now. "I was assessing how ready everyone was to leave and, well, how drunk they were. Afoniki was dancing with a girl, one of the debs."

"Debs?"

"Debutantes. She was too young to be dancing with a tiger."

"Could she have done it?"

Sarah didn't hesitate. "No way. I know—I knew her family."

That was an interesting switch. If you knew someone's family, that didn't change anything, did it?

"She's young, but not…bright." She frowned. "Or maybe she's too young to know who isn't nice and who is —a critical survival skill for operating in that world. Though he should never have been there. Afoniki I mean. Not that he couldn't afford a ticket, but why a breast cancer fundraiser?"

"It doesn't seem like something he'd be interested in," Cal agreed. The low light of the room and her voice had him settling deeper in the couch. The light was kind to her, but he knew she didn't need kind. She had a face that a guy wanted to go home to—he cut that thought off. She was Ben's girl.

"I wonder if he was trying to adjust his image or something. He's been at several fundraisers lately." She looked up suddenly, her smile wry. "Not that I was at them except when I was working. But I hear things…"

"Did you talk to him?" Cal asked, then wished he hadn't.

"He usually oozes up to me if he sees me." She made a face.

"He does?" Cal's brows shot up before he could stop them.

"Well, I met him during that whole business with Nell. I think he likes to ruffle my feathers. Liked to, I mean. Maybe it was a bad-guy thing."

No, it wasn't a bad-guy thing. There was something

about Sarah that made you want to draw closer. Was that why he'd avoided this until now? Kept his distance? Not good to pine for your brother's girl. He shifted uncomfortably.

"I'm sorry Ben had to work tonight."

Sarah's eyes widened. "Why?"

It was his turn to look surprised. "I thought—" He stopped. He'd already put his foot far enough in his mouth.

Sarah chuckled. "It's actually your brothers being…funny."

"Funny?"

"Well, think about it. If everyone thinks they are—let's call it competing for me, for lack of a better term—then no one is likely to notice what they are really doing."

Cal straightened and his nose might have quivered a bit. "What are they really doing?"

Sarah hesitated.

"You have to tell me now." Cal leaned forward, his feet planted on his side of the coffee table.

With a sudden movement, she leaned forward, her feet settling on her side of the table. Mischief sparked in her eyes and erased the shadows.

"Frank is heavily involved with a lawyer he met when he was testifying. An opposing lawyer."

"No way! Frank?"

"The one and only Frank," she said. She wriggled her shoulders. "She's a redhead and gorgeous, but wow, what a temper."

She must have seen Cal's eyes dart to her now-red hair because she grinned.

"A real redhead," she said, flicking the ends of her hair, "not this. Though," she added, "the red was there, I just brought it to the front a little more."

A lot more, but… "I like it," he said. "Liked the blonde, too," he added hastily. "Why—" None of his business why.

"I was in a weird mood when I had my last haircut." Her grin was a mix of rueful and wicked.

He chuckled. "So…Frank's redhead?" Talking about her red hair made him feel a bit weird.

Her eyes lit up. "She's keeping him on his toes. I'm sorry, I know he's your brother, but it's kind of hilarious. And I can't tell you how fun it is to finally tell someone."

She talked with her hands, sometimes with her whole body. The nails were neat, but they sported scratches and a couple of burns. Her kind of working hands, he decided, recalling the damage he'd accrued when he tried to cook.

Cal's shoulders moved in a sigh. "I need to see this Frank." What she described was not the brother he knew. He needed to see his brother's redhead, too. "How do you know so much?"

She laughed. "I told you I hear things. I'm the help, so no one notices me. And I met her once. I think she asked to meet me." Her chuckle was a bit evil. "He'll be lucky if he only gets singed a little there. Super-high maintenance."

"Frank's high maintenance." Cal tried to imagine how that would work out and couldn't.

Sarah gave a moue of agreement. "He's having to self-maintain with her. Wish I'd had popcorn. It was that good."

Cal laughed. "Man, I wish I'd seen." He settled his elbows on his knees, feeling faintly hopeful now. "And Ben?"

"Ben is a moving target." Sarah leaned closer, so that when the AC kicked on, the sweet smell of her flooded his nostrils. "Since Ben and I have supposedly been an item? He's been dating *ten* separate women."

"Ben?" Ben maybe logged a date a year until he met Sarah—who he hadn't been dating, Cal reminded himself.

She nodded. "It's like he fell off the date-watcher's wagon."

Carl rubbed his face. "I'm having a little trouble imagining my brother, Ben—" He stopped because he couldn't.

"I know, right? Looks so innocent. I saw him at one of my gigs and was like, hey, what's happening and it was like I was his priest. He wanted to keep it a secret, but he couldn't stand it anymore. You can't let him know I told you, because even though I'm not his priest or anything like that, it's pretty fun to be on the inside on this one. Since then, he's been keeping me updated. I keep waiting for the train to hit, but so far, he's just cruising along. And he keeps it low key. He only goes out once a week, so it's not like they can build great expectations on a date every other month, but still…a lot of variety." She must have seen the question he wanted to ask, because she added, "I'm also on his Instagram. Yes, he sends me pictures. My phone's on the charger, but when it comes off, I'll show you."

Her face was alight with laughter, the events of the night temporarily forgotten, but what hit him the hardest —*she didn't care.* She wasn't involved with either of his brothers. He pushed that thought back, not sure what to do—if anything—with this new reality. He'd sworn off involvement with women, he reminded himself. They couldn't handle his job. And just because she wasn't dating either of his brothers didn't mean there wasn't someone in her life.

"I promise, not a word to anyone," he managed, as his thoughts shifted like plate tectonics. "If you show me the pictures and keep me in the loop," he added.

"Blackmail I can live with," she grinned. "And I'll admit, it's fun to finally share. Does that make you my priest?" She laughed, the sound stirring something in the depths of his mind. "I couldn't even tell Nell because she'd have to tell Alex."

"Alex wouldn't—" He started to object and then stopped. "He'd tell Zach."

"And that's like telling the whole family," Sarah said.

His gaze narrowed. "You have become wise to the ways of our family."

"It's easy to sit and observe when you're all together." The wicked was back in her eyes.

He chuckled. "Safer, too."

He realized that they'd each leaned closer, not close enough for touching, but close enough he could see into her eyes. He'd never been this close to her before. The sweet, female scent of her swirled around him, sending the longing rising inside him. The longing to belong, to be with someone who cared if he came home at night. To be wrapped in the sweet scent and soft body of a woman would be—

He inhaled sharply, deeply, trying to clear his thoughts, but it just brought more of Sarah's scent into his lungs and closer to his heart.

"Anyone else I should know about?" he managed to ask, his voice suddenly husky.

Her brows arched. "Should? Or want to?"

Want. So much want.

He'd held her hand earlier. Not held exactly, but her skin had touched his. His hand, remembering, sparked along his palm. He lifted his lids, almost ashamed. She'd nearly been assaulted tonight—

Her gaze caught his and held it, the laughter fading to something else. Not desire, not yet. Maybe not ever. It should have been cold water in his face, but there was kindness in her gaze and curiosity. Some uncertainty.

He could lean forward and remove it—but should he? She deserved someone who could commit if things worked out. Someone who could have the talk about where their relationship was going. And he? It was easier to don SWAT gear and face down guns than risk that kind of hurt again.

He cleared his throat. "I…want to know if you have

any more dirt on anybody," he admitted. The temperature—at least inside him—went down some, though not as much as he'd have liked. The smile came back into her eyes—though it didn't chase out the curiosity. This was a woman who saw more than she let on. He needed to not forget that.

"Well," she said, leaning back again, "let me see…"

Chapter Four

SARAH DIDN'T REMEMBER FALLING asleep. She did remember waking a couple of times in a panic and was glad the light was on. And that Cal was there. His nightmare tip worked pretty well. Or maybe it was because she could see him when she turned her head. Was it possible for a man to sleep sexy? It worked in romance novels, but Sarah's real life had been devoid of male sleepovers. Not unlike the Bakers who didn't drink because of a drunk driver, Sarah slept solo because of her parents. It was possible she had as many—or more—trust issues than the Baker boys seemed to have.

People made assumptions about her—all except Nell who'd been her college roommate before she'd moved in here. It was mostly the hair, though her name and her family reputation probably played into those assumptions that she had an active dating—and sex—life. Like she had time for dating. Or sex. Most of her business happened during dating hours and she was exhausted by the time the sex hours rolled around.

She turned on her side, tucking one hand behind her head, and studied Cal. This was, she decided with some surprise, a first. Not exactly waking next to a guy but as close as she'd probably get to it. It was like that, but without the morning-breath worries.

The lower half of his face was shadowed with beard and ridiculously long lashes lay on cheeks chiseled by genes and hard work, she supposed. He'd been an inspiring sight in his SWAT gear, but now he inspired her…differently.

The borrowed sweat pants rested low on his hips, which allowed her gaze to drift up and study his chest. He wasn't overly "pec'd," but she could tell he kept himself fit. The muscles were there. He was long and strong, but what she found herself thinking about, for the most part, was the look in his eyes last night as they'd talked. He'd managed to make her laugh and it had felt so good. She felt a weird sort of melting sensation around her heart as she studied him.

He had a good sense of humor, and his kindness, well, she'd known the Baker boys were the good guys, but good encompassed a lot of territory. She'd known guys who did the right things, knew what they were and yet didn't understand simple kindness. Guys who were so busy saving the world they didn't have time for kind.

Sarah knew Cal was divorced. She knew he didn't like to talk about it, that he'd been hurt but not surprised—according to his sisters. None of the Bakers had illusions

about how tough it was to be the spouse of a first respon-
der. Sarah had been a bit scathing in her thoughts about
the former Mrs. Cal, but after last night? Something
about having a gun stuck in her face for the first time had
—as it should—given her an opportunity to reassess her
views on a variety of things.

Marriage was an act of hope in the best of times. An
act of defiant bravery in others, her thoughts going to
Nell and Alex. Nell's mostly dodgy relatives and his job
could still divide them. They knew what and who were
aligned against them but they were, according to Nell,
stronger together and hanging on tight. They weren't just
hoping it would work, but fighting on their own sides
for it.

To herself, Sarah could admit she'd had her doubts
about Alex and his ability to commit, but he'd stepped up,
been not just the hero who saved Nell's life, but the hero
of her heart.

The hero of her heart. Sarah considered the words. She
wasn't sure she'd believed in love, truly wasn't sure she
believed in it for herself. But watching Nell, and her
sisters-in-law, Hannah and Laura, find love might have
made her a little wistful. And this morning, wistful felt a
little more, almost reaching the longing stage. She'd
enjoyed the few dates she'd had with Frank and Ben, but
neither of them had made her feel any real longing for
more.

And here she was, after one scary night with Cal…
it was the stress, she decided. The scary stuff, the
commotion, his dramatic arrival all decked out in

SWAT stuff, that had done it. And his kindness, she reminded herself. A kind person was dangerous, too, in a way. Without meaning to, they could stir unintended hopes. And longings. Her free hand curled and then flexed as she remembered Cal's hand covering hers last night. The comfort and warmth she'd felt at his touch.

Heady stuff, touching. Was that what had driven her parents to such extremes? When they'd lost the ability to comfort each other, to be kind to each other, had they sought it from others? And, like addicts, failed to find the precise comfort they needed? For the first time, she felt… sorry for them instead of angry.

And perhaps, she felt a little sorry for herself.

She abruptly shoved the light blanket off of her legs and scrambled up. She hesitated, her gaze lingering on Cal's peaceful visage. They were good-looking boys, but Cal might up the game a little in that area. The firm, yet tender curve of his mouth. The strong jawline. The strength and goodness in his face. A sigh might have trembled out and she turned abruptly away, heading for the door.

She might have had a near-death experience last night, but she still needed to do a post-event assessment— this time a damage assessment. What equipment was still part of the crime scene and when would she get it back— if she did? What needed to be replaced in the event they held on to it for a long time…

At the door, she couldn't resist a quick glance back. After all, she might never have this chance again—but he made a movement, as if he were stirring, and she slipped quickly out.

CAL GROANED, rolled over—and fell off the couch with a thump that rattled the room.

Couch?

He rubbed his face and looked around. Oh right, couch. Sarah's. *Sarah?*

His gaze lighted on the empty couch, the pillow still holding the shape of her head, the blanket tossed to the side. He tensed, then realized he heard the creak of stairs out in the hall. He scrambled up and made it out in the hall in time to see her pajama-covered legs with exposed bare feet go out of sight.

He leaned against the doorframe and rubbed his face again, felt the scratch of early morning beard and not-enough-sleep thick brain. He should get his stuff and head home, but he hesitated in the hall. New Orleans didn't have cool mornings this time of year, but the cool from the air conditioning had settled in overnight, thanks to the sun giving them a break. The shadowed cool of the entryway felt good. And if he went upstairs—he needed a few minutes to wake up, collect his thoughts before he came face-to-face with—anyone. Figure out why he felt so unsettled and restless. And not exactly unhappy.

His team had done good last night. A clean in-and-out with no shots fired. There'd be less to explain during their official after-action assessment, though Big Chip

would be annoyed Cal hadn't waited for permission to
enter…not that he'd said anything when Cal told him he
was driving Sarah home—

His car. He'd tossed the keys to BuzzKill. It was probably parked outside Cal's apartment by now. Or would be
at some point. Didn't matter. It wasn't here. Which meant
he needed a ride to leave. Who could he call? Any of his
siblings, and he'd have to explain how he ended up
spending the night there.

He glanced up the stairs. There'd be no quick exit,
then. Not that—he just wanted a shower and a shave and
food. Because there wasn't any food here in a caterer's
house, he scoffed at himself. He just wasn't ready to face
Sarah's clear, deep-seeing gaze, he admitted to himself.

There was a knock at the door behind him, then the
doorbell chimed. It was a really highfalutin' sound. He
hesitated, but he thought he heard the shower, or at least
water running, overhead.

Two steps took him to the door, the floor cool against
the bottom of his bare feet. He fumbled with the lock for
a minute, then swung the door open and came face-to-
face with Ben. His brother's brows arched so high, they
almost reached his hairline.

"Hello," Ben said, the single word carrying a buttload
of assumptions.

Cal stepped back, gesturing his brother in. Words
crowded his brain, explanatory and defensive words, but
he held them back. In his family, it was better to say nothing. Talking just got you in more trouble.

"Sarah?" Ben asked.

"In the shower," Cal brought himself to say, even though the words made it worse.

His brother's gaze tracked down Cal's bare chest to the low-riding sweats and then back up again. The brows were still scalp-high and Ben's eyes were frankly curious.

"Nell and Alex are in Mississippi," Cal said. As terse explanations went, this wasn't his best.

"Oh." He could see Ben add this morsel to last night and the curiosity eased some.

Ben hesitated and Cal knew he wanted to ask, but wouldn't. He didn't.

"I need to get her statement."

Cal gestured toward the room where they'd spent the night. "You can wait in here."

He followed Ben in, knowing he'd note the separate couches and the signs of restless sleep.

More of the curiosity eased when Ben turned back to him. "How is she doing?"

"She was pretty shaken up last night." He hesitated then added, "I haven't seen her yet this morning."

Ben's gaze turned speculative and the silence wasn't comfortable. Cal felt no need to do something about that. He wanted to go upstairs and shower, but he also didn't want Sarah to come down and find Ben here. Until Sarah told him Ben's secret, he'd have felt like he had to leave— now he felt like he shouldn't. Even though he wanted to leave. His lips twitched as he remembered the ten women his brother was dating, but he wouldn't say anything. Ben would know who told him and the intel would dry up. He studied his brother's face, noting the signs of tiredness pulling at the edges of his eyes and mouth. Of course he was tired. He'd had to stay later than Cal had.

"Any idea who did it?" Cal asked, breaking the silence.

Ben's sigh told him more than the shake of his head. "The murder weapon mostly melted. It had this stuff in its core, but the surface—"

"Melted?" Cal's brows shot up now.

"Apparently there was an ice sculpture with some sharp shards. Whoever did it, used one of them."

"Surely, someone would notice anyone grabbing the ice sculpture," Cal objected.

"Late night and most of the remaining guests were drunk."

"But Afoniki's bodyguards—"

"Were watching him, not the ice sculpture," Ben pointed out. "Either he got stabbed while he was on the dance floor or just before."

"Before?" Cal's brows weren't getting a chance to lower.

"ME says it's possible he didn't know he'd been stabbed."

So the medical examiner wasn't their sister, Hannah.

"But—" Cal stopped. The idea seemed crazy, but he'd seen perps keep coming after getting shot. Cops shot to stop, not because they wanted to kill, but they had to keep shooting until an attacker was stopped—one who could cover seven yards a second, even when wounded. "It seems more a killing of opportunity than a hit," he said instead.

"We can't rule out the possibility that a hired hitter saw an opportunity and took it," Ben said. "Afoniki had a lot of enemies."

"You think a hitter disguised as a deb took him out?" Cal tried not to sound incredulous.

"A deb?" Ben's brows arched again.

"Debutante," Cal growled. "Sarah said he was dancing with a…deb."

"Well, if his dance partner is a secret hitter, that is the best disguise ever," Ben said with a grin.

"Sarah knows her family," Cal said, a reluctant grin punctuating this.

"Sarah knows everyone," Ben said.

"Not everyone," Sarah objected.

Both men swung around to find her standing in the doorway, her arms crossed, a shoulder propped against the frame. Her gaze flicked between them, the cool amusement making Cal want to shift from foot to foot.

"I came to get your statement," Ben said.

"I'll go shower," Cal said, though his gaze lingered on her for longer than it probably should have. Today she was undoubtedly the cool drink of water Frank had called her, even with the red taking over from the blonde. She'd pulled on shorts and a tee shirt, leaving a lot of skin bare. Cal, his throat dry, moved to the doorway. She flattened against the jamb so he could pass. He had to turn sideways to do it, leaving them face to face for a heady moment. As he moved clear, his heart pounding made his ears ring—but not so loud he didn't hear Ben say, "My little brother played protector last night, I see."

He didn't hear Sarah's response, if she offered one, as he took the stairs two at a time.

BEN HAD GONE and Sarah had moved to the kitchen by the time Cal thumped down the stairs.

"I'm in here!" she called, when the footsteps stopped. "The kitchen," she added, when the footsteps didn't start up.

He probably followed his nose rather than the sound of her voice. She'd put some bacon on. Apparently being held hostage by thugs and then grilled by a cop made her hungry. And she guessed that Cal was hungry, too. She might feel a bit guilty about not offering to also feed Ben, but two taciturn men in her kitchen was a bridge too far today. And she might feel a little guilty for ratting Frank and Ben out to Cal. Not enough to quell her grin at remembering the look on Cal's face. And it had been killing her, not having anyone to talk to about the pair. Okay, *gossip*. It was gossip pure and simple and she tried not to, but wow, especially Ben and his women-juggling. And she'd bet Cal didn't talk to himself outside his head unless absolutely necessary.

Her grin was still there when Cal appeared in the doorway. She kept it there to hide the sudden flutter of her heart at the sight of him. What was it about a cleaned-up good guy that made a gal's heart go pit-a-pat? He'd shaved, too, the air catching his brother's aftershave and bringing it her direction. Funny it never smelled that good on Alex.

Cal looked around and then asked, "Can I help?"

Wow. "There are plates and cups in that cupboard, silverware in the drawer there," she indicated both, then turned to flip her eggs. Her back to him helped a little with the heart rate issue, but even the bacon couldn't completely suppress the clean-guy smells. She heard the toast pop up and Cal moved to take care of it without asking. Nice.

In a few minutes, she slid eggs onto both their plates, added bacon and then went to join him on his side of the island. The stools were placed so that their shoulders rubbed together. Funny she'd not noticed that before. The intimacy of it was unsettling, but it was too late to move without it being weird, so she sucked it up and dug into her food. The silence was comfortable. Was this what it was like for Nell? Sarah tried to quantify what this was and couldn't, other than—comfortable, with an odd feeling of being more alive than usual.

"This is good," Cal said, rapidly clearing his plate.

Sarah shifted a couple of her strips of bacon onto his plate with her knife and he gave her a quick, grateful glance. When he finally leaned back, he sighed.

"Thank you. I—thank you."

"You're welcome." She pushed her own plate back and downed the rest of her juice. It did make one feel less hollow. Giving her statement to Ben had brought last night back to the front of her mind. The food helped push it back again.

"I realized you didn't have a way home after I got in the shower," she said. "And then I forgot again and let Ben leave, but I'm happy to run you home any time you're ready."

She wasn't ready to be alone yet, but he'd done more than she'd had a right to expect.

He opened his mouth, but before he could speak, the front bell rang again.

She gave him a wry look. "I don't usually get that much front door action." She pushed back and stood up. He hesitated, then followed her out into the hall, stopping a little behind her as she reached for the door and pulled it open.

Sarah had a feeling she should know the woman standing there on her stoop. She'd seen her somewhere— her eyes widened. At Nell's wedding. This was one of Nell's unfortunately-connected-to-crime cousins. She was dressed in tragic black, like a widow, with lace hanging from her sleeves and from the handkerchief she used to dab at her flawlessly made-up eyes.

"I'm Mirabelle St. Cyr," she said. "May I come in for a few minutes?" Her gaze tracked past Sarah and found Cal, widening in sudden interest—the male/female kind. Her chin dropped and she heaved a wan sigh.

Sarah stepped back and gestured her in, giving Cal a puzzled look behind the woman's back. His lips twitched and he gave a slight shrug.

The black-clad figure paused in front of Cal.

"You're a Baker, aren't you?" Her tone said it was a pity, as her eyes raked him from top to toe, then lifted her tragic gaze to meet his.

"Calvin, ma'am," he said.

"Ma'am. How quaint." She shifted her focus off Cal with obvious reluctance to ask, "Is there somewhere we can talk?"

"Do you want me to..." Cal began, but Mirabelle reached out a hand and let it touch his arm.

"It's not terribly private."

The faintness of her voice appeared to indicate she needed a seat, so Sarah led her down the hall to the more formal parlor. Cal glanced around this much less comfortable space, and then, after the ladies had taken seats, cautiously lowered himself into a chair. He looked relieved when it didn't collapse.

"What can I do for you, Ms. St. Cyr?" Sarah asked. She was beautiful, if a bit Morticia Addams with her clothes and makeup. Her eyes were pale blue in her porcelain face and the lips a discordant slash of deep red.

The red lips parted as if in protest, then compressed for a few seconds before opening once more. "Miss Burland, isn't it?"

Sarah nodded, repressing a twitch of lips at the "miss."

"Not many people are aware that Dimitri and I were going to be married." There was a flutter of black as a long narrow hand—with red-tipped nails—lifted the handkerchief to touch one of her tearless eyes.

Sarah felt her eyes widen, not in surprise exactly. More from the memory of Afoniki's actions his last night. Not that she figured a crime dude was a good candidate for fidelity.

"No," she admitted, "I didn't know." None of which explained the crime gal's presence in her parlor.

"I just wondered—the police have been so cagey about it all—how he…died? If he suffered? Who…?" She stopped and her cold, pale gaze met Sarah's. "If he said anything before…?"

"I…" Sarah had to stop herself from looking at Cal. "I honestly don't know that much, Ms. St. Cyr. I was the caterer, not a guest." She knew not to tell the deadly-looking beauty what Afoniki was doing when he died. His dance partner did not need that kind of attention. She was already traumatized enough.

"Oh. So you don't know if—" she stopped.

"If?" Sarah prompted, even though she knew she shouldn't. Did Mirabelle think Sarah knew if it was a hit or not? Seriously?

"You're sure you didn't hear anything?"

"Just some screaming," Sarah said.

"Dimitri *screamed?*" She looked honestly astonished.

"No, the women who saw…the blood," Sarah said, feeling a bit mean all of the sudden.

"Oh, that." She rose to her feet. "I'm sorry to have troubled you."

And now she felt less mean.

"Not a problem. I'm sorry for your loss," she said, trying to sound as if she meant it. She walked her to the door and saw her out, turning to face Cal who had also walked into the hallway.

"I wonder what that was about?" Sarah sort of knew the story of a crime boss who had left his crime empire to three of his henchman, an Afoniki, a Calvino, and a St. Cyr. Since then, the three families were said to have jostled for ultimate control of all of it, both by killing and by marriage. Nell was the result of a sort of Romeo and Juliet alliance of a Calvino and a St. Cyr—hence the cousin appellation—but Mirabelle was not the head of her family. No, that title went to her creepy uncle Claude.

"With that bunch, it could be anything," Cal said.

He hesitated, and Sarah found her insides tensing at the prospect of being left alone. But once again, the doorbell chimed.

"Seriously, it's not usually Grand Central Station around here." Sarah wasn't that surprised when she yanked the door open and found Cinzia Calvino on her stoop.

Cinzia was hot where Mirabelle had been cold. She was lush, brash, and voluptuous, a wholly sexual creature. When she stepped in, without waiting to be asked, she pushed back the shadows and the cool, bringing all the heat of a New Orleans summer day with her. She stopped when she saw Cal, her gaze also raking down and up him. Her red—a somehow sexier red— lips curved up and she smiled in an overt invitation.

"Which one are you?"

Cal might have sighed. "Calvin, ma'am."

"So polite." A blood-red nail reached out, trailing lightly down his chest before getting caught on the waistband of his jeans. "Such a waste." She sighed and turned back to Sarah.

Cinzia was also dressed in black, but it didn't drip, it

clung to each luscious curve of her figure. She was brown where Mirabelle had been black, but she was also all heat and restless energy. She paced further in, then turned, her gaze sweeping the space.

"I'd heard this was a nice place. Don't suppose you want to sell it? The location is amazing."

"No," Sarah said calmly, amused despite her distaste for tacky beauty. "Was there something else you wanted?"

She saw Cinzia's eyes flick in Cal's direction, and heard her wistful sigh before she turned to Sarah.

"I was told you were there when Dimitri died. I wondered"—her thick lashes swept down then lifted in a calculating gaze—"if he had any last words?"

"Last words?" Sarah said blankly.

"For me, his intended. Something that would allow me a…claim, since he didn't have an heir."

"You were engaged to Dimitri…?" Sarah managed not to add, "too?"

"And a devil of a time I had getting him to say the words," she said, without rancor. "I hate to see all that effort go to waste."

"I'm sure…" Sarah's voice trailed off. She didn't dare look at Cal. This was not the moment to burst out laughing. She managed to get herself under control. "I was the help last night. I…don't know, I didn't hear anything." She stepped to the still open door, holding it suggestively, though she wasn't sure the hint would be enough. Cinzia had some brass ones.

Cinzia hesitated, then managed to give a smile that

was almost nice. "I guess you're not the kind one could persuade to have heard anything."

It wasn't a question, but Sarah answered it anyway. "No, even if Cal wasn't here." She also didn't mention all the people closer to Dimitri when he'd died. No reason to sic her on them. They'd also been traumatized enough last night.

Cinzia sighed deep enough to almost explode her girls out the top of her bodice. She flashed Cal a lascivious look and then strolled out, her hip action...impressive. Sarah pushed the door closed once the bad girl had cleared it and then leaned against it, almost dazed. She looked at Cal, the amusement in his eyes starting a little flicker of warmth around her heart.

"I'm glad I don't have to go to that funeral," she said.

"If they'd been there last night, it would have been easier to narrow the suspects," Cal pointed out.

"I wonder why they weren't there?" Sarah mused. Was this the real reason Afoniki was at a breast cancer awareness fundraiser? To avoid his fiancées?

"You hadn't heard anything about the engagements?"

"No," Sarah shook her head, "but I'm not sure I would. They don't exactly run in the circles of my clientele." And former friends, though to be fair, not all of them shunned her. They just didn't openly seek her out. She thought about Maisie's "save" when Afoniki was bothering her. Maisie was the exception to the secret friends thing, but then Maisie could do what she wanted. When she grew up, Sarah wanted to be Maisie.

"Are you all right?" Cal's voice broke into her thoughts.

"I'm fine," Sarah said, her lips curving up in a half grin. "We've probably run through all the possible fiancées, don't you think?"

"All that I've heard of." He appeared to hesitate, then said, "You want to go somewhere? Or do you have to work?"

She could always find work to do. "Somewhere?"

"Where there isn't a doorbell. Away."

This time she didn't hesitate. "Yes. I would like that very much."

"My car," he began.

"I also have a car. I'll even let you drive it." That would make her dad roll over in his grave again, and if her count was right, that would put him temporarily right side up.

The way Cal's smile crinkled the skin around his eyes —and what that made her feel—should have given her pause, but she'd almost died last night. She'd lived, so she should *live*.

Chapter Five

CAL HAD GIVEN her an incredulous look when she handed him the keys to her dad's Hummer. She wasn't sure what he'd expected, but it wasn't that.

"I never met your dad, but…" he stopped, so Sarah finished it for him.

"When he bought this I realized that you can never really know someone, or their secret desires. If you'd asked me, I'd have said the only thing he ever worried about was getting kicked out of his Krewe."

"Could this do it?" Cal walked around the vehicle, letting one hand trail along the side as if he couldn't quite believe it.

Sarah shrugged. "I doubt it. It's a manly car and they were all about being manly, even wearing dresses for some Krewe thing. I used to wonder…"

"Used to wonder…" Cal prompted, stopping his circuit in front of her.

"If I was adopted. Or dropped on their doorstep."

Sarah grinned, even as the old pain tugged at her insides. "I used to wish I had a sister, one who might be more compatible with their hopes, or to prove I wasn't the only annoying daughter in the world." Nell had somehow known, even though she got on great with her parents. Of course, in the end Nell had found out they'd lied to her. Maybe it was dysfunction calling out to dysfunction. They'd been sisters from the moment they met.

"Parents are complicated," Cal said.

Sarah looked up and found his eyes kind. "That they are." He had a whole different level of that, she knew, from listening to Alex. Twelve siblings and a complicated dad. "You all make me feel better about myself," she said, with a slightly evil grin.

He chuckled. "Glad we could help."

He pulled open the door and jerked his head toward it. Sarah clambered ungracefully in. She should have thought about that when she grabbed the Hummer keys. When he was seated across from her, he shoved the key in the slot and gave her a look.

"Let's go find your somewhere," she said.

———

SARAH DIDN'T SAY anything when he turned the Hummer south. It was a little wide for New Orleans streets, but it did make the other cars move out of his way. He liked that. He took the turns which gradually took them down along the Mississippi on a long and narrow road that eventually reached Venice. He was tempted to drive all the way there, but he wasn't sure either of them had that kind of time. Still, it was a soul-calming drive with land and water in almost equal parts on either side of them.

The sky was a pale blue, streaked with clouds—lots of clouds—but so far no sign of an afternoon storm. He stopped in La Hache and got them fried shrimp, fries, and cold soft drinks, and they pressed on.

Sarah didn't talk much, other than the occasional question or comment and didn't seem worried by the silence. He gave her a quick glance, reassured by her contented expression. He found a wide spot to pull over so they could eat. There wasn't a lot of traffic along the road this time of day.

The food was messy and delicious, and the cold drinks went down just right in the high, hot sun. They sat on the hood of the Hummer to eat, leaning against the front window. Too many fire ants on the ground.

"I don't want to go back," Sarah murmured, as she pushed her cardboard tray of shrimp tails to the side. "If we stayed right here, eventually the stars would come out."

"And the swamp mosquitoes," Cal felt compelled to point out. There was enough wind coming off the water to keep them down for now. "But I like the concept." At some point, they'd have to drive back. She'd go her way and he'd go his. This felt like stolen time—but he'd like to steal more.

Sarah's chuckle was soft and the sound of it felt like it danced across the exposed skin of his arms—and then got under it. It was not good to let her get under his skin. There was no future for him with any woman, he reminded himself, surprised he needed the reminder.

"How are Alex and Nell doing?" he asked, as if the question flowed from the thought.

"They are good," Sarah said. "I worry about them having enough privacy living with me, but they say they're good. And it's a big house."

Cal hesitated. "They must have a few things to work out."

"Everyone has things to work out, I'd imagine," Sarah murmured. "They are good together."

"Does she worry…" he didn't finish the question, not sure how to phrase it.

Sarah's head turned his way. "Worry? Oh, you mean about him being a cop?"

Cal nodded.

"I suspect she does. Kind of ironic that your dad survived all those years and, well," she stopped, giving him an anxious glance.

"My mom and Helen," he said slowly. Strange, he'd never thought about it that way.

"Do you remember…them?"

"Yeah, my mom a little. I was four. Helen died when I was thirteen."

He waited for her to say it was a tough age to lose his mom, and Helen had been a mom, though he and his brothers always called her Helen. The girls reminded him of her. Instead of words, Sarah's hand covered his briefly.

The ensuing silence was comfortable. Overhead a

plane circled almost idly, then headed further out on the Gulf.

Sarah sighed and half turned toward him, and he felt his insides tense a bit.

"Don't you think those two wisegals' visits were a bit odd?"

Tension left him abruptly and he shrugged. "They are a bit odd."

"Yeah, but this time they were like caricatures of wisegals. They weren't that weird at the wedding, and they had to have tag-teamed outside. There wasn't time enough between the two visits for them not to see each other."

He stiffened again, but for a different reason. It was odd. Why had they both shown up like that?

"They both wanted to know if he said anything," he said slowly. Were those two up to something?

"It must get old having the family business only go to the boys," Sarah said. "But they weren't there at the party. And how would taking out Afoniki help them? Sounded like they were hoping for a marital takeover."

Were they rivals—or allies? Cal considered this and then finally shook his head. "I can't imagine how that helped them, other than calling attention to themselves."

"It does seem anti-wise, whatever, to do that," Sarah agreed.

"They could have changed their tune when they saw I was there," Cal mused, though he still couldn't see what they hoped to accomplish. This was why he liked kicking down doors. It required a different kind of thinking.

"It's nice," Sarah murmured.

"What is?"

"That you are all honest. I mean, this is New Orleans. My parents were…well, they had what I'd call situational honesty. As far as I know, they never broke the law but…" she stopped.

Cal glanced at her, but her lashes were lowered behind her sunglasses. Her hands were clenched in her lap, though.

"Their friends never assume I'm honest. I've always wondered if that's why" —she hesitated, then finished in a voice wiped clean of warmth— "that's why Dimitri's uncle first approached me to cater for him. I wondered if…"

Instinctively, Cal covered her clenched hands with one of his, his arm going around her back. "Don't. Don't wonder. It won't change anything, and you'll never know for sure."

She'd stiffened, but he felt her slowly relax against him.

"You're right. Of course you're right." He felt her deep inhale, then exhale, then her face turned up to his. Her glasses still hid her expression and her smile was tense, but it was a smile. "Thank you. I should get it stamped on a tee shirt or something."

That last remark held real humor, if a bit on the wry side.

"Is that what girls do these days?" he asked, hoping to get the humor going. "Helen was always stitching things on pillows and stuff and putting them in our rooms. She had a lot of hope."

Sarah's smile widened into something that dang near stole the air from his lungs. "My mom had people for that."

Now Cal laughed too, and somehow, in the laughing, his arm got further around her. It didn't even scare him because it felt so right. Only thing that would have been better was his mouth against hers. He looked at her mouth, grateful for his sunglasses that hid from her what he wanted, what he wanted so much it might have been a need.

It was only the unexpected sound of a car pulling to a stop behind the Hummer that stopped him from turning thought into action. He half turned to look, but the profile of the Hummer was too high. He felt his spidey sense tingling, and turned, the weapon he always carried appearing in the hand no longer cupped around Sarah's waist.

Doors opened. There was the crunch of footsteps and then a man came into view. He heard Sarah's sharply indrawn breath and he might have echoed it.

The intruder was a younger version of Dimitri Afoniki.

Maybe in his late twenties, Cal decided. He moved, trying to keep Sarah behind him, though he knew they'd be easy to flank. The two bodyguards he could see stayed back, their hands clearly in view.

"I wish only to speak with you," the man said, half

turning to survey the empty horizon, "though you have made that challenging."

"Who are you?" Cal said, his neutral tone surprising him.

"I am Pavel Afoniki, the cousin of Dimitri. You, I only know you are a Baker, but the Miss Sarah, Dimitri has spoken of you to me."

"Yay," Sarah said with a noticeable lack of enthusiasm. "I was kitchen staff. I don't know anything."

"You misunderstand my presence," Pavel protested. "It is to thank you that I sought you out."

He'd followed them for miles to thank Sarah? Cal didn't snort, but it wasn't easy.

"To thank me?" Sarah sounded surprised, but also skeptical.

"I have spoken with my cousin's escort team," Pavel said. "They credit you with preventing a larger tragedy from occurring." His cold gaze flicked to Cal's face. "And possibly saving their lives." He paused, his gaze returning to Sarah's face. Admiration didn't warm his gaze at all. "You kept your head in difficult circumstances."

Sarah slipped off her sunglasses and Cal was startled by the cool neutrality of her gaze. He'd hate to have her look at him like that. After a pause long enough to make someone with more of a conscience uncomfortable, she said, "You're welcome."

Pavel nodded, the slight smile on his lips interesting. Cal couldn't tell if it was interesting-good for them or interesting not-good.

He nodded. Cal thought he was going to leave, or maybe he hoped, but Pavel wasn't done yet.

"May I ask you a question, Miss Burland?"

"You can ask," she said, "but I reserve the right to not answer."

"That is fair."

Neither bodyguard moved in a threatening manner, so maybe it wouldn't get ugly.

Pavel glanced out into the wetlands for a moment, the breeze picking up the blond hair and ruffling its carefully smooth surface.

"Do you think one of them did it?" Only when the question was fully out did he turn to look at her. His gaze was still cold and dead, but not dangerous, more curious, Cal decided.

Sarah was quiet for so long, Cal wasn't sure she planned to answer him. Finally, she stirred next to him, swinging her legs down so they hung next to his on the side of the Hummer.

"I don't know who killed him," she said, "but when… they were positioned against the walls watching. It was a party. And my job was to keep the food table stocked. If you want my opinion, which is not worth much—no. They didn't do it."

There was a long silence and this time Pavel looked the other direction. "Who do you think did do it?"

This time, Cal decided Sarah was ready. "I've had a lot of time to think about it and I still come up with I have no idea. There was no one there, no one near him— most of the people around him were drunk by that time."

"Or appeared to be drunk," Pavel put in.

"You don't understand," Sarah said. "There were no…outsiders. And I say that as an outsider who used to be an insider. There were a bunch of…spoiled kids and an old couple."

"How old?" he asked swiftly.

"In their nineties," she paused. "He might have been a couple of years younger, but if I had to say who was holding who up? She probably was." Pavel's face still looked grim, suspicious. "If he'd been whacked with a handbag, she'd be your gal."

"If she was so…old, why was she still there?" Pavel asked, as if she didn't matter.

Cal felt a chill for the old lady.

"Because she's on the committee that organized the event. She never goes home until it's over."

Cal didn't sense any uneasiness in her voice, just amused patience, but he felt Sarah's hand clasp his. No way did she want to be the one who sicced this guy on an old lady.

"Then she might know who did it?" Pavel suggested. "Old ladies are nosy and see what they shouldn't."

"If she saw anything, then the police know it," Sarah said firmly. "If I were you"—was there a suggestion of relief she wasn't?—"I would let the police do their job. They are very good at it." She paused, then added, "At least then you'd be sure you had the right person."

"And if they fail?" Pavel said, his skepticism apparent.

Sarah was quiet for another long stretch. What could she say to that?

"Well, if anything happened to anyone from the event, the police would know who to ask about it, wouldn't they?" She held Pavel's gaze, though her grip on Cal's hand got almost painful. "It seems to me that it's in your best interest to let them do their job."

"And what should I do?" There was some scorn in his tone, but Cal saw respect in his eyes.

"Well, if it were me, I'd plan a funeral." She paused again, and then spoke, her tone less neutral, almost kind. "I've lost family and I know it doesn't seem like enough. But it's really the last service we can do."

There was a long silence, but Cal sensed the menace had eased. Finally, Pavel nodded.

"I am sorry that I interrupted your picnic, is that not what you call it?"

"It is," Cal said.

"It is a nice place to be alone."

Cal didn't see a signal, but somehow the bodyguards moved into action, opening the car door for Pavel and then sliding into the car with him. It took a bit of backing and forwarding to turn on the narrow road. Cal didn't relax until the dark car was a speck in the distance.

"Well, that was odd," Sarah said.

"He's already read the witness statements," Cal said. It made him coldly furious that it was so, but Pavel had the resources and there were always those willing to be bought. Sarah was right about that. It helped to know who the good guys were. And sometimes it was only family a guy could trust, he mentally added, thinking about his dad's old partner.

Sarah didn't seem surprised, but then she'd grown up in New Orleans, too.

"I wonder if the wisegals know about Pavel?" Sarah murmured.

"It's whack-a-mole with these guys," Cal muttered. He dropped off the side of the Hummer and helped Sarah down, then gathered up their trash.

"We better head back," Cal said. He'd never have brought her out here if he'd had any idea they were being tailed. He opened the passenger door for her. "Did you know Afoniki had a cousin?"

She climbed in, shaking her head. "I tried not to know things about him."

Smart girl.

Chapter Six

THE SILENCE during the drive back was less comfortable than the drive out had been. Sarah kept her mouth closed for fear of asking Cal to stay with her again tonight. Call her a wimp, but three visits by suspected crime figures made her a mite uneasy. She'd seen the word "adulting" on Facebook the other day, as in "adulting is hard." Today, she couldn't argue with that. Looking back, she could see where she'd had to adult a lot, since neither of her parents had worried too much about being the adults in her life. Even their deaths in a drinking/speeding accident had been adolescent. If she hadn't been managing their finances for them, she'd have been a lot worse off.

Today, she didn't want to adult. She slanted a look in Cal's direction. He was big and strong and *good* and she wanted him—on her couch, or rather on the other couch. That was all, she told herself. Now she felt the fatigue from last night trying to crest into a great big wave. She'd never been able to sleep in a car, but this might be the exception—except Cal had to be at least as tired as she was.

She shifted, trying to straighten the slump from her back and think of something to say that didn't sound begging or lame. She stole a look at his profile. Dang, the guy owned rugged. It was like he and the Hummer were made for each other. She was the one who didn't fit.

Well, it was time to start sucking it up. She cleared her throat, quietly though, and shifted so she half faced him.

"If you wouldn't mind going to my place first, so we can switch cars?" She drove the Hummer once a month around the block to keep it running. Did not feel comfortable driving it further, she was not ashamed to admit to herself. "Then I can run you home."

His glance was swift, but searching. "I can get someone to pick me up," he offered instead.

Which, she wondered, would give her more time with him? More time in a non-needy way. It was sad when she couldn't get a thought all the way out without a scoff attached. Really sad.

"Are you sure?" she asked, afraid the silence was too long. Had she taken a nap in there?

"I've got twelve siblings—all of whom owe me favors large and small." His grin was kind of heart-stopping. "And I think you're too tired to drive."

"True," she admitted, with a side helping of wry. "It's amazing how exhausting it is to be held hostage." Not to mention the restless sleep that followed. Cal had been right about the post-traumatic stress.

Then because the silence was suddenly too something,

Sarah leaned forward and switched on the radio. "Cupid" filled the silence. Not the song she'd have chosen to lead with. She'd turn it off if that wouldn't have been too revealing. And then it got worse when the song switched to Norah Jones singing "Heart of Mine." It could have been Sarah's anthem. It felt as if it turned over the need in her heart, putting it out there for him to see. She didn't —she couldn't look at him—not even a sneak peek.

How strange it was to suddenly feel the bite of longing, a bite both sharp and sweet. She'd dated, though not as much in the past few years. But she'd tried to find a yin for her yang, a significant other that wore well. Not once, in all those years, had she felt this pure longing, this bittersweet yearning to believe in love for herself. Why was it so easy to believe in what Nell and Alex had, in what Hannah and Logan had, even be happy for Zach and Becca. And Laura—well, she wasn't sure about Archie yet. He, not unlike herself, had some big shadows in his life.

Did that mean she believed in love? She considered this as the music shifted to "Say Something." How ironic was that? Say what? I want to believe? No, she did believe in love—for others. So why not for herself? The temptation, the longing to glance at Cal was almost overwhelming. Only her fear of what she'd see kept her gaze straight ahead. The bare coastline landscape shifted to outskirts of city, and then they were in the chaos of Saturday traffic. It was different from weekday traffic, or it felt different. Because it was Saturday traffic.

Sarah knew Cal was divorced, that he'd taken it hard.

She gave him props for not mentioning his ex. She'd quit counting the dates where all the guy could talk about was the ex—whom he was always totally over.

That was the main reason she'd pretty much given up on dating. It was so much work to care enough to try to connect with the other broken people in her dating pool. Being alone wasn't that bad—until a gun was shoved in your face and you wished you had a big, strong shoulder to lean on just until your own strength returned.

She would be all right. How did she know this? Because she'd been all right all the other times. She'd been alone that night she had to identify her parents' broken bodies. She'd been alone before that, stood alone on the other side of the chasm that had separated them as long as she could remember. The night they'd died? That might be the closest they'd ever been.

And she usually didn't feel sorry for herself. She was tired. Time for feet-planted, chin-up, digging deep.

Her timing was good as Cal turned into her lane and pulled the Hummer back into its spot in the garage. She slid out before he could come around and open her door. She dropped onto the broken pavement, taking a moment for the planting of feet. Her sunglasses still hid her eyes, so it was easy to produce her business smile.

"I can fix us a snack while you're waiting for your ride," she said.

Was his smile as facile as hers? She didn't know him well enough to tell, but it did seem lighter on the charm.

"Sounds good," he said.

Sarah had barely dropped her purse on the kitchen counter when the doorbell chimed.

"You have got to be kidding me," she muttered. Even during business hours, her doorbell didn't ring this much.

She wasn't surprised Cal followed her out into the hall —and boy, was she glad he had when she swung the door open. At first she didn't recognize him, though she knew she should. The man on her stoop was thin and gray, both hair and skin. He reminded her of that guy on *The Simpsons*, the one with the pointy nose—Mr. Burns, only Mr. Burns had more color in his skin. Sarah knew the suit was good, so it had to be his frame that made it hang badly. He'd have been a bad caricature of something except for his eyes. She'd looked in a few bad-guy eyes in the past few days and this guy might have won a bad-guy-eyes contest. She did not have words for how much she wanted to slam the door on those eyes.

She felt Cal shift so that he stood just ahead of her, filling the doorway and partially blocking the sight of creepy guy.

"St. Cyr." Cal's voice was cold enough to put icicles in the August air.

"I don't believe we've met, though you have that Baker look," St. Cyr said, his voice an almost comic contrast to his creepy vibe. It was the whine and the pitch. They were both wrong for an uber-bad guy.

St. Cyr? Sarah frowned. If he was related to Mirabelle St. Cyr…wow.

St. Cyr ignored Cal, extending a hand that looked a bit like a dead fish. It felt like one, too, when Sarah automatically lifted hers so that his could close around it. A faintly musty odor filled the space between hot and cooler air.

"Claude St. Cyr," he said, his voice a little more nasal as he tried to be polite—or so she supposed. "And you are Sarah Burland." The thin mouth turned up in a parody of a smile. "I did try to call." He half turned his head and Sarah realized two big bodyguards flanked him on the stoop. One held a bunch of daisies.

Daisies. As in pushing up daisies…?

The ham fist was thrust out as St. Cyr angled his body so he didn't touch them and they didn't touch him.

Sarah accepted the bunch, though she wasn't sure she should.

"Thank you?" She couldn't help making it a question. It helped tamp down her "what the—"

"I was grieved to hear of your upsetting experience."

That voice was so wrong on so many levels. The urge to giggle tickled her throat and she coughed. He immediately stepped back and lifted a handkerchief to cover his mouth and nose.

From behind the white square, he said, in a now muffled whine, "If there is anything I can do to help, I hope you will let me know."

Yeah, that would happen.

"Thank you," Sarah said again. This time her cough was on purpose and totally fake.

St. Cyr backed up some more, almost falling off the edge of the top step. His bodyguard gripped his elbow, hard enough to make the bad guy wince. As he spun around, he jerked to an awkward stop.

"Ms....Daigle," he gasped, his voice breaking into a falsetto in the middle.

There stood Maisie Daigle. Her expression was flinty.

"Claude." Ice dripped from Maisie's voice. She backed up just enough so that Claude and his bodyguards had to edge past her.

Yes, even the bodyguards edged past, the twice-her-height bad guys. Maisie maybe reached to their belly buttons.

"I think I'm in love," Cal murmured in her ear, causing Sarah to choke again.

This sent Claude scurrying to his car where he almost dove inside. Maisie turned to watch the bodyguards scramble in, too, then the car squealed away.

"Who is she?"

"Maisie." Sarah moved out onto the stoop, her arms out. Maisie stepped up and into the hug. This close, she felt so frail, mostly bones, but she smelled like Maisie—a mix of powder and elegant scent. And Maisie returned the hug with almost equal strength. Sarah released her and half turned. "I'd like to introduce you to Cal Baker."

Maisie's head tipped to one side. "Yes, you look like a Baker."

Cal grinned, despite the considering tone. "Yes, ma'am."

"Cal, this is Maisie Daigle—"

"If you say anything about my stalwartness or position, I'll never speak to you again, my dear," Maisie said, her papier-mâché mouth curving into a smile as she briskly shook Cal's hand. "Nice to meet you, young man."

Cal took this reduction in age and status well, though Sarah noticed he was also careful not to look amused. Of course, he had just seen Maisie reduce a wiseguy to about an inch tall.

"How did you do that?" he asked, awe in his voice.

Maisie's smile might have been a bit self-satisfied. "I had an encounter with him when he was in kindergarten." As if that explained everything.

And in a way it did. She'd probably seen him wet his pants. That had to change things.

"He's not a nice man, and worse, he's annoying," Maisie summed him up. "Why was he here?"

Mutely, Sarah held up the daisies.

Maisie's brows rose sharply and then she reached out, lifted the bundle from Sarah's hands and tossed it over her shoulder.

"Now, my dear, I came to see how you were after last night."

An old hand gripped Sarah's elbow and steered her firmly inside. Somehow Sarah found herself in the parlor with Cal seated gingerly on the spindly chair next to hers. Feet planted, brave face made no difference to Maisie. She gently extracted the night and day's events, then gave Cal an approving look, though she also expressed concern about the sudden influx of wiseguys and gals.

"At least Guido hasn't shown up yet?" Cal pointed out and got a concerned look.

"I so wish you had not said that," Maisie said in a

gently reproving tone. When Cal started to protest, she lifted a bony finger. "They watch each other, you know. He will come to make sure he didn't miss something." She gave a tiny sigh. "Bad men are so predictable. Sadly, if you step on one, another crawls out of the woodwork."

"Well, hopefully you won't run into Pavel," Sarah said, leaning forward to pat the old hand on the old knee. "Bet he never went to kindergarten."

"It is hard to see them as children, isn't it?" Maisie said, getting that dreamy, looking-back expression.

Sarah exchanged a look with Cal that might have asked without words if he still loved Maisie. He may have nodded without actually nodding. Sarah might have sighed, wondering if she needed to be ninety before someone fell in love with her.

"You will be fine, my dear," Maisie said, rising with surprising grace to her feet.

Sarah believed her and nodded. One didn't not believe Maisie, not in New Orleans anyway.

Just then, the doorbell chimed.

"That'll be Guido Calvino," Maisie said with an impish smile.

GUIDO CALVINO DIDN'T STAY LONG when he saw Cal standing at Sarah's back and the old lady behind her. It seemed the old lady was right. They were all watching each other and trying to figure out if they'd missed something.

"There's one thing I don't get," Sarah said, when she closed the door on the smooth-talking, too-polished wiseguy with the gentle old lady trotting off behind him as if she was herding him away. "Well, one thing among the many."

Cal hiked a brow. Truth to tell, he was whacked. Even his blood corpuscles were tired.

"It makes sense they are all watching each other and stuff, but why did Mirabelle come in the first place?"

It was a good question. And one he had a feeling the old lady hadn't missed either. Still feeling his way to an answer, he asked, "Do you have any sense of who might have done it?" The words came out more murmur than real question, but it had kind of been the theme for the day.

Sarah didn't say anything as they both made their way back to the kitchen and the snack she'd promised. Or so he hoped. He found it encouraging when she headed for the fridge. Almost absently she began to remove things, setting them on the island. She paused long enough to hold up a soft drink, and when he nodded, she handed it across to him. He could use the caffeine. As he popped the top, he noted her expression. She was seriously considering his question.

"I wish I could see a list of the people who were there," she finally said. "But I'm not sure it would help. The obvious answer is one of the bodyguards."

"But you don't think one of them did it?"

Sarah paused, her knife over two slices of bread. Finally she sighed. "I don't think the one I talked to did it.

He was pretty freaked out for a bodyguard. I mean, you pay someone to watch your back, you expect them to keep their cool, you know?"

Cal nodded. "Why do you think they lost it?"

"Well, one minute their guy is dancing, and the next, he is facedown in his own blood, still..." She finished putting together a hefty sandwich and shoved the plate in Cal's direction. "Still, that can't have been their first dead body." She frowned as she started to work on a sandwich for herself. "My sense was they were—or he was—afraid. Of retaliation, maybe? And things spiraled into a Charlie Foxtrot?"

"Maybe the Charlie Foxtrot got a boost from the killer?" Cal suggested, in a pause between bites. Man, the gal could put food together. He hadn't noticed her doing anything that different from what he did, but the taste? He'd never achieved anything like this. Between the food and the caffeine, life began to return to his cells and sinews.

Sarah's brows arched. "That's a possibility." Her frown lines deepened—without reducing her cute factor —as she considered this. "And kind of a relief," she admitted. When Cal raised an brow because his mouth was full, she added, "I was starting to get a little paranoid about the party guests. For a minute, when Maisie showed up here..." she broke off and gave a rich chuckle.

Cal almost choked on his food before he managed to swallow the bite and laugh. Then he sobered, studying the last of his sandwich. "That's why they came to you."

He lifted his lids to meet her gaze. "You were sober, you're observant, and you have a brain."

"Well, thank you, I think," she said, "but how would the wiseguys and gals know that?"

He grinned. "Well, they do have their ways, I would imagine."

"If they have their ways, it should have led them to Maisie. Her knowledge of that social circle is wide and deep and there's not much she misses—though I hope they don't bother her," Sarah added.

"If she'd seen anything it would already be in her statement," Cal pointed out. "I think they were looking, or hoping, for the things you remember later."

Sarah sank onto a stool and leaned her elbows on the counter. "It's weird, but it seems more hazy, less sharp with each hour, and I find myself questioning what I thought I knew. The order is less clear, too."

"It happens. You think you'll never forget and then it starts to fade. That's a good thing," Cal added. "Your brain's way of protecting you, but it makes it tough in court."

"Well, I hope I don't end up in court," Sarah said.

For the first time, Cal noticed how blurred the edges of her smile were. She was exhausted. She needed to rest, but would she? Alone in this big house? He hesitated, not because he didn't want to stay, but because he did want to stay. He…liked her. He'd noticed her around. How could he not? She was a beautiful woman, but he'd avoided getting close, getting to know her, he realized. He'd avoided most women since his divorce, but he'd avoided her…more. All the walls he tried to throw up, all the excuses were just gone.

He liked her. Okay, nothing scary there. She was nice, smart and funny. Not just a pretty face. And she needed help. She hadn't asked, which he respected.

"I could doss down on the couch again tonight," he offered, working at sounding casual. If anyone was watching, they'd know he hadn't left. Considering the way the men had looked at Sarah, he didn't mind if they jumped to the wrong conclusion—though Sarah might mind.

But the relief in her eyes and smile erased that worry. Of course, she might not have realized someone might be watching her.

"Are you sure? I'll admit I wasn't looking forward…" anxiety was in front of the relief.

"Don't mind at all." The words were a little too emphatic but maybe she hadn't noticed. A smile bloomed on her face, erasing anxiety.

"Thank you. So much. I know the couch—"

"It was fine," Cal said. His back might not completely agree, but most of the rest of him was on board.

Chapter Seven

AFTER THE PARADE of bad guys and gals, Sunday brought
a trickle of Bakers, as the word filtered out through the
family ranks. Hannah, who had almost been blown up
but found love. Laura, who'd also been held hostage and
found love. And head of the family, Zach, with his love,
Becca, who had almost been killed with him.

Sarah was starting to see a pattern—though hers
didn't have a whiff of romance yet. She'd probably jinxed
herself by talking the bodyguards off the ledge. She was
so excited for Nell and Alex to get back, since they'd also
faced peril and found romance.

In addition to sharing their peril stories, Cal's siblings
and parent had studied him covertly and then asked
pointedly about Ben. It had been so tempting to out him,
but Cal had been watching, so she'd held her tongue and
provided snacks and drinks. Sibling politics were still
pretty new to her. If he didn't want to take the cheating

heat, he could tell on his brother. And there was no question the food helped take the edge off the disapproval.

She met Cal's glance over the top of his dad's head and saw something in there that put some heat into her cheeks. It wasn't a come-on look. No way he'd do that in his dad's presence—at least she didn't think so—but it was odd. She could identify awareness, but the rest of it baffled her. Cal was an enigma wrapped in some yummy.

Not all of Cal's siblings showed up. Some were working. But the texts were flying. She heard the dings of group texts hitting phones in the background. There was almost a rhythm to it.

And then Nell and Alex walked in. Across the crowded kitchen, Sarah saw Nell's brows rise and Alex almost broke out in expression. It was a near thing but he managed to hold the line.

Apparently no one had texted them. The swivel of heads between her and Cal and them made her wonder if it had been planned this way. Television was pretty dull in August.

"Did someone forget to invite us to the party?" Nell asked, her tone mild, but her gaze meeting Sarah's with some concern.

Nell knew they shared some overwhelm where the Bakers were concerned. Part of the joy of each being an only child. At least Sarah had slept better last night. Cal was almost as good as a security blanket, though one without the hugging. But his solid presence had helped her get larger chunks of sleep, which in turn had helped her with today's onslaught.

A silence formed around Nell's question. Apparently no one wanted to be the one who explained. Or they were giving it over to Sarah as the person involved. It didn't matter. Sarah wasn't ready to talk about it. She felt an inner tremble if she let herself think about it for too long. Mentally, she could dance lightly around the situation or focus on the side issues, but when she moved into the heart of it—yeah, she might start crying, which would be so embarrassing. And do a lot of damage to her cool-under-fire image she'd worked so hard to cultivate.

She managed a light—she hoped—smile. "I'll tell you later," she said. Or she could just pull up the article online and let her read about it.

Maybe one of the Bakers had the same idea, because both Nell and Alex's cellphones pinged. Laura and Hannah both rose and started to gather up dishes. Zach? Well, he did his usual stoic statue impression. She should study his technique. She had a feeling she was going to need it. Soon, she decided, as both Nell and Alex glanced down at their phones, did double takes and then started reading.

Well, it saved her having to make explanations. She couldn't even exchange a glance with Cal, not with all the eyes on them. Over the rattle of dishes, Sarah caught the word "Ben," and sighed. He owed her. Big time.

THE ROOM HAD MOSTLY CLEARED of Bakers, though they'd all left behind an air of the "other brother" disapproval. Cal could only admire Sarah's self-control. If it had been his secret, he'd have outed his brother without hesitation. It was a sibling-eat-sibling world when you had twelve of them. Probably the only one who hadn't gotten a text update was Ben.

Alex was still in his mulling stage, added to which, he was in a difficult spot. He wasn't Sarah's big brother. And Cal had done his job. And if he thought Cal was treading on Ben's toes, he couldn't say so in front of Sarah. That was one of the first rules of sibling club—you don't talk in front of non-family.

Nell moved over next to Sarah and clasped her hand. "You okay?"

Was there a bit of tremble to Sarah's smile?

"I'm fine. Cal's been looking out for me so I wouldn't be alone," she said, her gaze lifting to slam into Alex's.

Nothing like taking the fight to the big brother. Cal suppressed a grin and avoided his brother's gaze. There was a small silence that Nell broke.

"I wonder what will happen to Dimitri's…business?" she asked.

"Apparently there is a cousin or something," Sarah said.

"How—?" Alex began and then stopped his gaze moving between them.

"We kind of met him," Sarah admitted. "His name is Pavel and he looks like a younger Dimitri."

"Met him?" Alex's voice was the scary quiet one.

Cal didn't shift on his stool but it wasn't easy.

"Your…cousins stopped by, too," Sarah said. "Apparently wiseguys and gals are as nosy as regular people."

Nice deflection. Give the gal a medal, Cal thought appreciatively.

"What did they want?" Nell asked, glancing at Alex.

"Well, Mirabelle and Cinzia let me know they were both engaged to Dimitri and wanted to ask if I knew who did it," Sarah said.

Both Nell and Alex's brows shot up.

"Well," Alex said, not sounding unhappy about this.

Everyone waited for more, but it didn't come. Alex picked up his soft drink and drank deeply, then lowered it and realized everyone was looking at him.

"What?" he asked.

Cal looked at his watch. "I need to go." He knew there was regret in his voice. This earned him a long look from Alex, but Cal had a lot of experience enduring Alex's long looks and just waited it out. Finally Alex nodded.

Cal turned to Sarah but found he didn't know what to say. Oh, he knew what he'd like to say, but he couldn't say it in front of Alex and Nell, even if he managed to say it.

Sarah rose and crossed to him, going up on her toes to kiss his cheek. Her scent surrounded him, going deep into his lungs and her words sunk sweetly into his heart.

"Thank you. I…thank you," she said, stepping back.

There was something in her eyes that made hope want to get a foothold, but he didn't do hope—did he?

He told himself that, but he didn't believe it. On the

side away from Alex and Nell, Cal touched her hand and nodded. For an instant, a smile flickered on her mouth. Then the lips firmed. He nodded once more, then turned and left.

Chapter Eight

It felt kind of deja vu. It was another party. A different venue but almost the same crowd. No ice sculpture this time, though. So, it was almost the same, but not. It felt the same, though. Except not.

Sarah realized that the difference was inside herself. Normally, she got a bit buzzed from the process of catering an event, from seeing the food roll out smoothly, seeing the food consumed, watching the overall event happen—just the whole process. People liked her food, even the snooty ones, because the food disappeared off the tables. It helped that this was New Orleans—a city where people liked to eat and weren't embarrassed about it. Even a poor person could eat well in New Orleans.

If she didn't look past the venue—more ritzy this time with the columns—the scene was almost the same as it had been a week ago. People talking while the band played soft jazz in the background. There was no dancing tonight, but the crowd ebbed and flowed from the polite networking, the pull that kept the tide in motion.

The smells were different this week because the menu was not as heavily New Orleans, but her food always smelled good. It was a key part of the experience and it tended to cover the heavy perfume smells. There were fewer unfortunate body smells, but the rich weren't immune to getting and sharing their BO. And if they were rich enough, everyone else ignored it, too.

Maisie, with Valentin at her side, was at the center of one swirl of people, but that wasn't unusual. And so far, there'd been no wiseguys or gals—that she'd seen. And none had bothered her all week. Hopefully, she was done with her dance with the wise devils.

On the surface, her life had returned to normal. Her staff had come through last week in pretty good shape. They'd started out the night a little tense, but had gotten into the groove faster than she had. She felt off, an observer more than participant. She'd spent more time watching people, too, though she'd never left a server empty. It seemed she could do some of this on automatic. She just didn't like automatic. Part of the joy for her was being in the moment, with maybe a touch of the conductor for her little orchestra.

It could be her imagination. No one had said anything to her. She hadn't even got any concerned looks after the first half an hour.

She felt the lack of Cal in her life. There, she'd admitted it. She missed him. Two days with the guy and she had withdrawal. How long would it take for her to get over two intense days together? Two days against the rest of her life. It should be easy. They hadn't even held hands. She covered her hand where his had brushed against hers as he was leaving. It was as if her skin couldn't forget.

She needed to get back inside her own head, inhabit her own body, and get on with her life, her business. She'd worked too hard to let it all go to crap because some idiot shoved a gun in her face. For heaven's sake, Baker boys had swirled through her life since Nell met Alex. They were just variations on a theme. Her mind produced the words and her heart flinched from them. Well, the truth hurt, didn't it? Cal was definitely a more interesting variation on that theme.

She gave herself a mental shake and ran an eye over the tables, looking for anything that needed addressing. Looked good, but the desert table would need restocking soon. She half turned to head back to the kitchen and heard a voice behind her.

"Sarah."

She stared straight ahead, counting to five before she turned around. She felt the wave of his too-strong aftershave assail her nostrils.

"Hello, Basile," she said. "I haven't seen you around for quite a while."

He smiled, the white of his teeth so much neater and straighter than the last time she'd seen him. His tan was a bit much as well. He was handsome in a plastic way, like a television game-show host. Even the humidity couldn't discourage the upward lift of his perfectly sculpted dark hair.

"I've been busy," he said, his tone suggesting he could say so much more about that, but chose not to.

Thank goodness.

His gaze did a visual assessment of her, with enough lascivious in there to be offensive. Before she could move out of range, he took her hand in a clammy clasp. It felt like her skin actually shrank from the contact.

"The one that got away," he murmured in what he probably thought was a sexy tone.

He'd always been touchy-feely in a creepy way. Sarah couldn't understand how come he'd never targeted her mom, at least not to her knowledge. Men always seemed to miss the creep factor, but Basile had put his hands on her Mom, too. Maybe her creep-o-meter got dulled by alcohol. Or she hadn't had one.

Instead of noticing how much Sarah disliked Basile, they'd pushed her to marry him. She'd lost track of how many times he'd proposed—with an air of certainty that she'd eventually give in. Because who didn't want to be married to a handsy creep? Of course, that had been when he thought her family had money. After the accident, he'd oozed in other directions.

She stepped back, so that he had to let go or be thrown off balance. She'd perfected the right distance to make it hard for him to crowd her space. Practice makes perfect.

Why did women put up with it, she wondered, not for the first time. Why did she put up with it? It was partly manners, she knew. Predators picked their locations. He knew she wouldn't make a scene here, not with her business on the line, even though she wanted to. Almost dying made it harder to be polite, she decided. She wanted to slam the heel of her hand into the practiced smile and the worked-on aquiline nose.

She wanted it so much, she had to clasp her hands together to hide the tremble. Perhaps something flashed in her eyes, because he took a step back. Sarah smiled, the not-nice one. She'd planned to make an excuse but she didn't. She just looked at him and waited.

With an air of having just discovered someone he had to speak to, he turned and disappeared into the crowd.

"Who knew it was that simple?" she muttered.

"Every woman should have a look," Maisie said. "It saves so much unpleasantness with types like Basile."

Sarah turned and grinned at the old lady.

"No one ever told me that," Sarah explained, "but I will be refining it going forward."

"You have the potential to be formidable," Maisie said, her tone almost considering.

Oh great. No wonder she couldn't get a date with— she stopped the thought. She was moving on from that. She supposed that becoming Maisie wasn't a bad goal. She'd have to do it without the super-rich husband. Get rich on her own. And old. So she didn't have to decide tonight. But she might need a goal that didn't involve kissing a Baker boy.

Maisie moved to Sarah's side, her gaze sliding over the milling guests.

"I didn't know he was back," Sarah said, not asking, but if anyone knew why Basile was back, it was Maisie.

"His fourth wife got the chalet and enough alimony to keep him local for the foreseeable future."

"Great." Still, Sarah didn't have the money to tempt Basile. Maybe it was "the one that got away" factor. Or he'd just been slithering past because that's what he did.

"It is a pity," Maisie agreed. Her gaze turned toward Sarah. "How are you doing?"

"I'm fine," Sarah said automatically, then felt her lips twist wryly. "But this fine is different than before."

Maisie nodded. "Life is supposed to change us, else what's the point?"

She hadn't thought of it exactly like that, but Maisie might be right.

"I'll try to remember that," Sarah said, while hoping no one stuck a gun in her face again. That seemed like a life lesson she didn't need to repeat.

CAL WASN'T QUITE sure how it had happened, but he was back at his dad's house having dinner with him and his girlfriend. The twist? Ben and Frank were also there. It was obvious they were as surprised as he'd been. He was aware that Becca gave all of them surreptitious glances from time to time. Zach? His glances were not surreptitious and were familiar. Their dad had a nose for knowing when something was going on.

The thing was, he didn't know what was actually going on, just what he thought he knew was going on.

It seemed the family had been fine with the friendly rivalry between Ben and Frank, but Cal getting in the mix was not okay. Maybe it was just a brother too far for them. If only they knew…

He glanced up and found Ben studying him with a hint of worry. He should be worried. The sisters would eat him alive for dallying with ten women. Cal returned to his brother a bland look that did nothing to dispel the worry—or answer his brother's unspoken question. When Ben looked away, Cal turned his attention to Frank.

Frank had spent as much time on his phone answering text messages as he had eating his dinner. Zach was showing signs of annoyance, but then Zach didn't know about the high-maintenance redhead. Cal knew exactly why Frank was keeping this one on the down low. Relationships had a better chance of surviving—or ending neatly—if the whole family wasn't in on it. Too many cooks spoiled more than the soup.

The devil of it was, he cared about every annoying one of them and liked hearing what was going on, too. It was the multiplication that made it hard—and made him a hypocrite.

"How are things going on the Afoniki murder?" Zach asked suddenly, breaking up a ten-minute stretch of silence.

Ben looked up, a fork halfway to his mouth. He lowered it back to the plate and admitted, "Not well. It's like a locked-room mystery, with too many suspects locked in there with the body."

Zach frowned. "Surely you can eliminate most of them."

"You'd think," Ben said. "I think one of the body-guards did it, but proving it? That's not going to be easy. If one of them got paid off, they hid the payment really well. And the other crime families claim they were getting along peachy good."

"Peachy good?" Zach sounded revolted.

"That would be Cinzia's words, not mine," Ben said.

"Cinzia told Sarah she was engaged to Afoniki," Cal said, absently. It took a few seconds for him to process the silence these words had triggered.

"She what?" Ben asked, carefully.

"She said she was engaged to him," Cal said again, adding, "but then so did Mirabelle."

"They both claimed to be engaged to him?" Ben was not doing well at keeping his voice even. Cal nodded. "And you only now thought to mention it to me?"

Okay, fair to be annoyed, but how was he to know neither of them would mention it? Was it only to wind up Sarah? Or entitle them to more information?

"I haven't seen you since last Saturday," Cal pointed out. They didn't normally see each other a lot, but Cal might have been avoiding Ben. And Frank. Not because he was afraid of what they'd do or ask—neither had grounds to question him—but because he was afraid of what he'd admit to knowing. It had been hard keeping the smirk off his face through this very long dinner. And several times he'd almost slipped in a jab or two during the normal give-and-take of the conversation. Keeping secrets was hard times thirteen.

He could tell Ben wanted to bust him harder, but it was an unwritten code not to bust each other in front of Zach. Of course, a diversion was the best option in this case.

"What did you think of the heir apparent?" Cal asked, his tone casual. Then he shoved food in his mouth.

"Who?" Frank got the question in before Ben because Ben also had food in his mouth. At least the question got his attention off his phone. Frank was part of the organized crime team at the FBI, so technically he should know this.

Cal took his time chewing and then swallowed. "Pavel Afoniki?"

Frank exchanged a look with Ben then said, "He's not on our list. When did he show up?"

Cal shrugged. "He paid Sarah a visit the day after the murder. Just like the others."

"That's interesting," Ben admitted, "but not sure it helps, since he wasn't at the party. I'll need to check in with Sarah to update her statement."

Cal saw the speculation in Becca's eyes.

"How is Sarah doing?" Becca asked, directing the question at Cal.

All of a sudden all attention focused on him. "I... don't know," he admitted, wondering why he felt such a stab of guilt about this. "I've been...busy." This sounded more lame than not knowing. Excuses were weak.

"She's working tonight," Ben offered, a hint of payback in the gaze he threw his brother before returning his attention to his plate.

Cal wanted to ask where, but he couldn't. Not now. Ben's knowledge had changed the balance of power. Cal could change it back with a word but it was striking from weakness. He could check in with Sarah, he realized, using Ben's situation as an excuse. She was almost his priest, after all. He suppressed a grin at the thought.

Becca's forehead wrinkled in concern. "I hope she gave herself enough recovery time."

"You gotta get back up on the horse," Zach said.

Zach had never been on a horse in his life that Cal knew. He opened his mouth to protest, but closed it again, settling for sharing a wry glance with his brothers that closed their ranks for the moment.

SARAH COULDN'T HELP the tension that began to rise inside as the end of the event approached. Was this a different kind of PTSD? Maybe PPSD—Post-Party Stress Disorder? Her staff didn't seem to feel it, chattering in the kitchen as things wound down. Smells that had been sharp and appetite-stirring were now a bit stale, and mixed with perfume and aftershave and alcohol.

Maisie and her gentleman escort of the evening left, Maisie pausing for a moment to give Sarah a royal lift of her hand in farewell. Her leaving precipitated the final breakup of the evening. The guests thinned fast after that, which meant Sarah could retreat to the kitchen and ramp up the cleanup. All of her crew, too, got the familiar second wind from seeing the finish line in their sights.

Whatever had separated her from her real life, paled in the face of hard work. It wasn't the "sweet spot" runners talked about. There wasn't anything sweet about dirty pans and greasy dishes, but there was satisfaction in getting the job done and done well.

She was…content, she decided.

Outside in the ballroom, the music faded. Sarah headed back out for the final clearing of the table, her gaze sweeping the room. The musicians were packing up their instruments. They'd make a pass through the kitchen for the food they knew Sarah had set aside for them.

The room was still a bit muggy from the crush of bodies, but the AC was trying to catch up, swirling the musty air rather than clearing it out. The room setup was not her purview, but she noticed that, other than removing the decorations, the cleanup crew wouldn't have too hard of a job. There were chairs out of place, of course, and the small area with tables and chairs was jumbled.

A lone figure was slumped in the corner, she realized. Somebody had gotten too tanked to get home. There were a few dishes on that table. Her staff would have waited until he'd left to do the final clearing. It smacked too much of rushing. But now he needed to be helped into a cab and sent home.

With a sigh, she headed over there, realizing with a strong sense of dismay, just who the malingerer was.

Basile Bonadventure.

Such a dashing name for such a small, petty man. In sleep, he looked even smaller. The tanned face sagged, with the mouth half open. At least he wasn't snoring. This wasn't the first time she'd had to shift a drunk, but she didn't usually have to do it at these more upscale dos. The attendees usually brought someone with them to do that for them.

She started to reach out to give him a shake, when something—perhaps the silence—sent a chill down her back that the AC couldn't match. Or perhaps it was his utter stillness. She studied him, realizing with another round of chills, that his chest wasn't rising and falling. Or moving at all.

It took everything she had to reach out toward the slack arm hanging off the side of the chair. As soon as she touched his skin she knew he was dead. The skin was chill and nothing like living skin.

With a shuddering breath, she circled him, looking for signs of violence. There were none she could see. He looked asleep—other than the part where he wasn't breathing. Maybe he just had a heart attack? Or a stroke? Despite the tan, he was—he looked to be in terrible shape.

Sarah backed away from him and turned, almost slamming into the lead singer from the band.

"Need help getting him into a cab?" he asked, like someone who also knew the drill.

Sarah licked her lips and gave a slight shake of her head. "He's…dead."

"What?" The singer took a step back.

"He must have had a heart attack," she said, not because she knew, but because she knew it would be easier to process for all of them. "I need to get my cellphone so I can call the police."

"The police!" He took another step back.

"It's procedure in a sudden death outside a hospital," she explained automatically. She saw his brows arch and added, "My roommate married a cop."

"Oh." For whatever reason, this reassured him. He cast Basile a doubtful glance. "Do you want me to wait…?"

"Come and eat your dinner," she said. "He's not going anywhere." Then she added, "Thank you."

"For what?" The young man looked startled.

"For being a gentleman and kind."

"Oh. Right. No problem." His shoulders were a little straighter as he headed for the kitchen.

AFTER ALL THE action on Frank's phone, it took Ben a moment to realize it was his own phone ringing. Cal was just pushing back his chair to leave, but he paused when Ben said, "Sarah? Everything—" He listened for what felt like long time, even though it was just a few seconds. Ben lowered the phone with a frown.

"Well?" Zach said impatiently.

"What?" Ben looked up. "Oh, that was Sarah."

Which they all already knew.

"She's well, she found another dead guy—not a murder," he added hastily. "At least, probably a heart attack. She wasn't sure who to notify. I told her I'd take care of it."

She'd called Ben, not him. Of course she had. They were friends. He'd thought—but he hadn't done anything. Hadn't even checked on her.

"I think I'll run over there," Ben said, rising.

"I'll go with you," Cal said before he thought.

Ben's eyes widened. Some others might have as well. Cal found he didn't care. Even if it was a heart attack, this was her second death in a week. Cal paused and turned.

"Thanks for dinner, Becca. Dad."

Frank and Ben echoed the thanks, Frank taking the opportunity to exit with them. Cal heard his cellphone ping as they left the house. Cal bit back the sardonic remark on the tip of his tongue as a thought hit him. Just because Frank and Ben knew they weren't dating Sarah didn't mean they knew the other *wasn't* dating her. It was an interesting twist if it turned out to be true. He needed to think about this later.

He climbed in the car beside Ben, half expecting questions, but none came. Of course they all knew that questions exposed what you didn't know, and in their family, not knowing could bite you in the butt. He had a question stuck in his throat right now: *How was she?* But Ben couldn't answer the question.

It felt like it took forever to get there, even though the streets were as empty as they got in New Orleans—except during a hurricane. The humidity put a halo around the streetlights as Ben drove as fast as he could. He could see the flashing lights down the street, and when they pulled up, he was surprised to see a crime scene rig outside. They exchanged glances and scrambled out, running up the steps, side by side.

Inside, Cal saw their sister Ingrid in her crime-scene gear bent over a body slumped in a chair. The investigator for the coroner's office was next to Ingrid, gesticulating about something.

Ben frowned and asked the question uppermost in Cal's mind.

"Why is a heart attack scene baked?"

IT WAS A NIGHTMARE, Sarah decided. She'd had a lot of them in the week following the hostage-taking thing. She'd wake up from this one just like she had from the others. She'd gasp for a minute, realize it was a bad dream, then get up to get a drink and let the sweat cool.

She recognized Ingrid, of course. Nell's sisters-in-law had been around more than the boys. She didn't recognize the coroner's office investigator, which kind of messed with her dream theory. Did she know what one was? Or what one did?

As if he sensed her confusion, he explained, "Normally, I wouldn't come out for something like this, Miss

Burland, but Bonadventure has some troubling contacts."
He was an older man with a jaded expression. "It does
appear he had a heart attack, but we won't know that for
sure without an autopsy."

Sarah vaguely remembered reading that autopsies
could be ordered for deaths outside a hospital, but they
weren't always because of money. The coroner's office
was seriously underfunded. The article, she recalled, had
said New Orleans was a good place to commit an Agatha
Christie-type of murder because the killer had a good
chance of getting away with it. Unless the corpse had
"troubling" contacts, it seemed. Her insides tensed
because her parents had done business with Basile, too.
But they'd been gone for four years. Whatever business
they'd had with Basile was long over.

"Do you think he was murdered?" she asked, so tired
she was surprised she managed the question.

"I couldn't say," he said, easily, even though Sarah
knew he could—and had said already by summoning a
crime scene team. "But thank you for not clearing the
table once you realized Bonadventure was deceased. You
might have made our job easier."

Easier if he'd been poisoned, she decided, amazed she
could think this. Apparently, the brain kept working even
when the body didn't want to. What she couldn't understand was why they seemed to suspect poisoning. Basile
was a jerk with "troubling" contacts, but he wasn't a
crime figure. At least, as far as she knew. Which wasn't
much. But they'd been onto it so quickly. So something

about Basile had triggered this response. The questions this time were different—and the same—as last week.

Finally they stopped and she was alone for a moment, alone at the right moment she realized, when Ben and Cal came in. Was this what she'd hoped for when she called Ben? But why would Ben call Cal?

Both men saw her and crossed over to join her on the opposite side of the room from the corpse.

"You okay?" Cal asked before Ben could.

She looked at Ben, then back at Cal. Did Ben know Cal knew? She couldn't tell.

"I'm fine," she said. "No hostage-taking this time." She tried to smile. Wasn't sure she managed it. She'd staggered past tired about an hour ago and was now trying not to face-plant into exhausted.

Cal's shoulders twitched and his hands curled into fists. The coroner's investigator saw Ben and signaled for him to join them, so Ben, after giving her a concerned look, left them.

The silence wasn't comfortable and it wasn't actively uncomfortable. But it wasn't easy like it had been last weekend.

"Do you know when they will let you leave?" Cal finally said.

Sarah looked up, trying to process the question. Finally she shook her head and rubbed her face.

"I'll see if I can find out," he offered. He hesitated, then asked, "Do you have someone who can drive you?"

She shook her head again. She'd sent her staff home

before the cops arrived. She and the event coordinator had been the only two to wait. "I'll be all right," she said.

"I rode with Ben. I'll drive you," he said, before walking away.

Sarah had to admit that, even as tired as she was, she wasn't too tired to enjoy the view. Cal looked fine in his jeans and close-fitting tee shirt. Cal almost caught her looking when he turned and came back.

"They said you can go," he said. "Do you have anything left to load?"

"No," she said, pushing herself upright with an effort. She and the others had busted a move to load the van. Sarah had worried that Basile's death might cast a shadow over her business, but he'd shown no signs of food poisoning. It was a bit odd he hadn't attracted any attention, but Sarah was also too tired to mull that. She was not a sleuth, nor did she play one on television. "I planned for a clean getaway," she said, managing a vestige of a grin.

Cal's hand closed on her elbow and she was grateful for it as they headed out through the kitchen, with a pause for her to collect her purse and keys, and then out where her van waited. Some more *deja vu* as Cal helped her in the passenger side and then went around to take his place behind the wheel.

He didn't speak until they were well on their way.

"Did you know him?"

"Sadly, I did." Sarah admitted, stifling a yawn behind her hand. "He was a…friend of my parents. I never liked him," she added.

"Yeah?" He paused for a light and gave her a quick glance.

"He was a creep. I never understood why my parents spent time with him, but there was a lot about my parents that I didn't understand." Wow, way more information than she usually handed out. She was tired.

Cal chuckled. "I feel your parent pain."

"Zach does have enigma down pat," Sarah said. She wanted to ask how he'd ended up with Ben tonight, but couldn't think of a way to ask it that didn't come across as nosy.

"Zach had Ben, Frank, and I over for dinner tonight," Cal said. He glanced at her. "Do they know about each other?"

She chuckled. "No, they don't."

"I just assumed they did."

"I probably shouldn't have told you," she admitted. "I feel like I've violated client privilege or something."

"That would be why I haven't used my knowledge for evil," Cal admitted. "But it's not been easy."

Particularly since his dad and siblings thought he was muscling in on his brothers' territory. Sarah felt a bit of heat in her face and was glad it was dark. Because none of them were muscling in on any territory that included her.

Darn it.

Chapter Nine

SARAH WAS UNCHARACTERISTICALLY LATE COMING down
the next morning. Nell was already up, her sketch pad out
and a soft drink next to her on the island's counter. Sarah
regarded her silently for several minutes, recalling Nell's
brushes with the dark side. She'd considered herself very
supportive, and she had done her best, but it looked much
different from this side. She sighed silently. She could tell
herself that this had nothing to do with her parents or
their past. She'd read in a book about a body of water
turning over, releasing toxic carbon dioxide into the air.
But her parents weren't a body of water, even if she
sensed them turning over in their graves more than once.
She told herself it wasn't happening, but it didn't take
away the worry that there was still muck to be exposed
about her parents.

At least no one could say she had illusions to be
dispelled. Though her unease said that might not be true.
Maybe she hadn't set her expectations quite low enough.

She sighed again, this time trying to draw in some resolve. The night hadn't been nearly long enough for a real recovery, especially when she wasn't sleeping that great.

"Morning," she said, breaching the kitchen and Nell's preoccupation. She didn't look directly at Nell, opting to head for the fridge instead. She felt Nell's scrutiny, but could only prolong the moment she'd have to meet her friend's gaze so long. Her fridge was far too organized. She lifted out a soft drink can and popped the top before making the turn, using the lifted can to stall some more.

Nell studied her for way too long and Sarah knew she saw more than most. She was an artist, even if she mostly drew vegetable and fruit characters for her children's books. Alex was lucky he had few secrets.

"What happened," Nell finally asked.

Sarah sighed for a third time—she needed to stop before it became an annoying habit—and sipped onto a stool opposite.

"It was another interesting event," Sarah admitted. Nell's eyes began to widen, so she hastened to fill her in.

Nell blinked a few times during the brief recital. Thankfully this time there wasn't a lot to tell.

"Did I meet him?" Nell asked when Sarah finished.

"I don't think so," Sarah said. "He quit oozing around when he realized there wasn't much money. According to Maisie, wife number four has left him." Four wives in just over four years was impressive in a bad way.

Nell's brows arched. "So he was…"

"A suitor? My parents' choice? I'm afraid so." She hesitated, but Nell was the one person she could tell.

She'd been there and had to deal with worse. "It's kind of creepy to have two men die not long after talking to me."

Nell nodded sympathetically. "More than kind of. It makes you confront your own mortality, which isn't that fun."

Sarah laughed, though a bit ruefully. "True dat."

The bell chimed. Sarah bit back this sigh and pushed back her stool. Hopefully, this was a customer and not a wise-someone or a cop. Unless it was Cal, but otherwise, customers only.

———————

AS ARRIVALS WENT, this one was a bust when Sarah opened the door to find Cinzia on her stoop. Sarah's expression must have been less than welcoming, because Cinzia's heavily reddened lips curved ruefully.

"Can I come in?"

Sarah stepped back and indicated permission word-lessly. She was afraid if she spoke, a sigh would come out.

"Who—" Nell's question cut off in the middle. "Cinzia."

"Nell."

If they'd been cats, their backs would have arched and hissing would have commenced. Since they weren't cats, they both murmured insincere greetings, while Sarah, after glancing outside for any other wise-people sightings, shut the door. She resisted the urge to lean against it—in lieu of a sigh.

As someone on Facebook had mentioned, adulting was the pits sometimes.

Sarah directed Cinzia to the formal parlor, as opposed to the comfy room she'd taken Cal to, but paused to catch a look from Nell, whose eyes were full of unspoken, but pointed, questions. Sarah shook her head and mouthed, "Run, save yourself." There was no reason they both had to suffer, and Sarah had a feeling Cinzia didn't want anyone else in the room with them.

Something to drink was offered and refused as Cinzia moved restlessly around the room picking small ornaments up and putting them down again. In addition to the red lips, she wore a toned-down red dress, one cut with swathes of black. Mafia mourning? She paused at the window, turning so that the light was at her back and highlighting the sweep of hair and ripely curved body. Her heels were probably registered as lethal weapons.

Her gaze swept the room before coming to meet Sarah's.

"It's the same as I remember it."

There might have been a question in the comment, but Sarah needed a moment to come to terms with the fact that Cinzia had been in this room before.

"Your parents knew how to throw a party."

Was she trying to be provocative? Sarah wasn't sure. With the light at her back, her expression was indistinct. She could have been stalling. Despite her air of assurance, Sarah sensed a rare uncertainty from her. Well, rare in Sarah's limited experience. She'd certainly managed to exude confident grief a short week ago.

Sarah decided to take the comment at face value—at least while in Cinzia's presence. She could angst over it later.

"My parents both had that rare gift of charm," Sarah said, proud of the evenness of her tone. "Everyone liked them."

Cinzia sashayed a couple of steps away from the window, bringing her face back into better view. "Everyone?" Her sharply marked brows rose. Before Sarah could respond, she added, "I liked them."

Sarah blinked. It was true that while Sarah had loved her parents, she had not liked them. She'd seen behind the curtain, lived there long enough to have no illusions left—or perhaps a few if she was surprised they'd known Cinzia. Or that Cinzia knew Sarah had not liked her parents.

"Why are you here?" Sarah found she'd lost patience, though the words sounded wearier than she'd have liked. One should not, she was sure, show weakness around this woman.

"Basile, of course."

"Basile?" Sarah repeated the name blankly. She hadn't forgotten last night, but Basile and Cinzia? She'd not seen that one coming.

"I need to know, was he murdered?" The words were direct, unusually so for her, Sarah guessed. "It's…important."

Sarah hesitated. Was there risk in giving this woman any information? Probably. But the truth was, she didn't know anything for sure.

"I don't know." When Cinzia started to protest, she held up a hand. "I really don't know. I thought he had a heart attack."

"But the scene was, how do you say it, baked?" Cinzia pointed out.

"That surprised me, too, though the police are called in when someone dies outside of a hospital or a doctor's care. It's standard procedure." Sarah would have grinned if she'd felt like it wouldn't be misconstrued. She almost sounded like a cop.

"It's not standard procedure to call in a crime scene unit."

Well, she probably knew better than Sarah. She almost repeated what that investigator had said about "shady" contacts, but stopped herself in time. Cinzia might have been that contact.

"I was surprised by that, too." And worried, if truth be told. What if they'd found something in her food—but if anyone else had gotten sick, she'd have heard by now. This was not about her, though the paranoid, tired part of her wondered. She had to bite back a "why do you care" question. Not her business. And she really didn't want it to become her business. If Alex had been there, he'd be puffing up like a big old tom cat. Sarah allowed herself a sigh. It felt indicated. "I really don't know anything."

Surely Cinzia had some dubious contacts inside the police who could give her something.

"Can you at least tell me what happened?"

So she didn't want to talk to any of those contacts? That's what it felt like.

Sarah motioned to a chair and sank into one without waiting to see what Cinzia would do. After a short hesitation, Cinzia sank gracefully into a particularly hard chair and did it without wincing. Impressive.

"There's not a lot to tell," Sarah said. "I didn't even know Basile was there until about halfway through the evening. He said hi and I——" She stopped.

"You told him to buzz off?"

The words sounded funny coming out of her mouth. One expected something more sinister. Sarah nodded wordlessly. She was developing a look. Would it work on Cinzia? Sarah considered the question and decided her look wasn't ready for prime—or wise—time.

"I've never been a…fan…" Sarah said carefully.

"You always were smarter than your parents."

How well had Cinzia known them? No, she wouldn't, she couldn't go there. That would start questions in her head that she could never answer. She sure wouldn't trust Cinzia to tell her the truth.

"We certainly had different opinions about some things," Sarah said carefully, "which is not unusual with parents and kids." She pulled herself back from this line. Cinzia was not interested in Sarah or her issues. "Anyway, I didn't see Basile again until almost everyone had gone. I thought——" She hesitated, but decided she didn't need to sugarcoat anything for Cinzia. "I thought he was drunk. I do sometimes have to hustle a guest into a cab."

"Really. How…interesting," Cinzia drawled, her lips curving in a smile that didn't reach her eyes.

It was strange, because she was so hot from top to toe—until Sarah looked into her eyes and found the North Pole—nowhere near Santa's workshop.

"I went over and realized it was Basile and—" Her throat caught for a moment as the scene came back to her, then she managed flatly, "He was dead. Cold."

"So he'd been dead for a while," Cinzia murmured. "Interesting."

How? Sarah didn't ask it out loud. She knew better, but her brain insisted on asking it anyway.

"You heard he was getting divorced again," Cinzia said still in a murmur, and then she looked up, as if she realized she'd prompted more questions than answers. "He asked me for a job."

Well, that didn't improve her opinion of him at all.

"Well, now you don't have to worry about it," Sarah pointed out, knowing worry was not Cinzia's problem right now, but willing to play "let's pretend" to get her out the door.

"No." Cinzia rose in an abrupt, yet sinuous movement. Her gaze acknowledged Sarah's "time to leave" hint. She looked around one last time, as if she didn't plan to be back. Then she smiled at Sarah, one devoid of charm and sincerity. "Thank you." She hesitated. "Strange how different you are from them."

There was a question in there—or doubt. "I'm told I take after my mother's mother," Sarah said. "She irritated my mother no end."

Cinzia nodded as if that explained it, whatever it was.

With some relief, Sarah closed the door on her unwelcome guest. This time she did lean against it, even though it was carved and not conducive to leaning. She didn't mind the mild pain. It reminded her she lived, she was awake, and there were worse things she'd faced.

And whatever her parents had gotten up to with Cinzia, it didn't matter now.

It didn't matter now, she repeated to herself.

CAL DIDN'T LIKE GOING to the morgue, even though they'd finally moved out of the funeral parlor and into the new building. Its function was the same: dealing with death. But it was the only way to see his sister, Hannah, who had Basile Bonadventure on her autopsy docket.

Funny how the smell wasn't that much better than the old place, but at least she had a proper office and examination room to work in. He wore his street uniform and no one stopped him as he came in. He found Hannah in her office, working on her computer, a pair of computer glasses perched on her nose.

He paused for a moment, remembering a younger Hannah learning to type because writing by hand was too slow. She'd always been too smart, so of course her brothers had helped her out by trying to make sure she didn't know just how smart. That hadn't always worked. She was smarter than them by a ratio he didn't want to know.

As if she sensed his presence, she looked up, a smile taking the serious from her face as she pulled off the glasses and stood up.

"Cal." She let his name hang there for a few minutes while she studied him. "Official business?" She was right to be puzzled. Cal didn't usually have official business with her office—other than providing her with the occasional corpse to dissect.

He hesitated. Hannah had a good nose for a falsehood. "Kind of," he said. "I heard you were doing Basile Bonadventure's autopsy?" He made it a question and a statement, so it sounded like he had a right to ask.

Her rising brows told him she hadn't totally bought that right.

"I just finished it." She gestured to her computer. "I'm working on my preliminary report. It won't be complete without toxicology," she added, as if anticipating his question.

"So no overt signs of foul play?" he murmured, cocking a brow in her direction.

"No."

"So why the big response? I looked up his record. He's small-time. Barely a blip on the bad-guy radar."

She hesitated, then gestured him toward a chair. But he noticed she closed her office door before sitting back down in her desk chair.

"This is not for sharing," she said, her fingers tapping against her desktop.

"It's big?" he asked, trying to figure out how.

"It's…" she sighed. "It's…puzzling. And could be a big pile of nothing. Or…" Her gaze got distant.

"Or," he prompted.

"Or it could be, well, it still won't be big, but it's not great for us, for the department. I mean, we already have a rep as being a great place to commit murder. So I actually hope I'm wrong. But if I'm wrong…"

"You've wasted resources and, what, they'll fire you?" The coroner's office had a chronic money supply problem.

"Not sure they could find someone to work for what I do, but I won't be in the popular column."

Cal grinned. "Is there a popular column?"

"Well, it's more like a 'you don't suck' column, but who wants to be in the 'you totally suck' column around here?"

She had a point, so Cal tried to look sympathetic. And tried not to look at his watch. Even he knew it would rain on the sympathetic look and shut off the flow of information—if that information actually started to flow.

"So what is this sinkhole you're trying not to fall into?"

Hannah looked up and sighed again. "So about six months ago I got a body in, someone who had died at one of these celebrity fund-raising things."

Cal sat a little straighter.

"Looked like a heart attack and I'd have probably passed on an autopsy, but his medical record didn't jive with a heart attack. My spidey sense quivered a bit, but"—she lowered her voice—"the boss was away, I was sick to death of bullets and stabbings, and I had an intern, so I thought, what the heck? So I ran a toxicology on him." She leaned back. "And then I started polishing my resume because I thought I was in for it this time."

She did have a rep for pushing boundaries and Cal wasn't sure the new boss knew how smart she was, but he'd bet there was a medical examiner or coroner somewhere who could figure it out.

"And…" he prompted again. Was this what pulling teeth felt like?

"His blood had high levels of aconite."

"So he was poisoned?"

"Well, there are some herbal remedies that contain aconite. There are a lot of accidental poisonings in Asia from it and the vic had traveled to Hong Kong recently. But it was interesting. Since the boss still wasn't back, I did a little digging, or rather, asked Logan to do it. The victim was not a particularly pleasant individual, but there was no obvious motive other than he was a bit of a creeper."

The tapping of her fingers sped up.

"I was preparing my defense when Logan said it reminded him of a case he'd investigated last year. Guy died of an apparent stroke at a big-do party."

"Poisoned?" Cal asked, his spine getting an inch straighter.

"No toxicology was done. Just a sense Logan had that something wasn't quite right. But no one cared. Again, a creeper with no clear enemies and family not interested in pushing for more information."

"And your boss is letting you run with Bonadventure?"

She made a face. "Not turning me loose, exactly, but willing to let me check this once."

"So if Bonadventure had a heart attack, you're done with the creepers?"

Hannah tipped her head from one side to the other, then finally nodded. "Pretty much."

"One 'maybe' and one 'pretty sure' is kind of slim," Cal said, with a frown.

"I might have done some further digging. It's not super easy, because these fundraising organizers don't like deaths at their parties getting around. But I found two more deaths, each about a year apart, that could have been suspicious. I might have sold them a bit, but if there is someone out there discreetly offing people, well, I'm impressed. No rush, very little fuss, and victims who aren't terribly mourned by their families."

"And someone who didn't let Afoniki's death put them off their schedule," Cal pointed out.

"I know." Hannah frowned. "Bonadventure might not follow the pattern—or what there is of a pattern. For one thing, it's only been six months. He only got back in town this week, so I might be worried. But I had to jump on it. Afoniki's death doesn't fit the profile, and not just because of who he is."

"He was stabbed," Cal agreed. The use of the ice shard could indicate a crime of opportunity, or someone who knew all about the sculpture. Based on Ben's level of frustration, they might never know which.

"With a fairly unique piece of ice, too," Hannah said, sounding a bit too impressed.

"What do you mean?"

"I had to do some research on ice sculptures for his autopsy. I had no idea how complex it all is. But apparently this particular sculptor used something called Icecreate." Before Cal could ask, Hannah added, "It's basically tiny pellets of dry ice that cements the ice together and helps the sculpture to retain its shape for longer. The actual design was approved by the committee in charge of the event, so someone could have planned to use it, but how could anyone be sure that Afoniki would show up and that they could get close enough to use the ice knife?"

"Which brings us back to a crime of opportunity," Cal said.

"Ben's getting a lot of pressure to solve it so a war doesn't break out between the families," Hannah said, "but I'd be surprised if we ever find out who did it."

Cal leaned back nodding thoughtfully. "And if your toxicology comes back positive?"

"Then I get to think up a name for my serial killer?" Hannah grinned.

CAL USED the drive to try to think of serial killer names. The words "patient" and "lazy" came to mind. What kind of serial killer only killed once a year—that they knew of, he reminded himself. Serial killers came in all types and sizes, from patient to impatient. But this one did appear to be remarkably patient—*if.* It was a big if. From the quick look he'd gotten at the corpse last night, Bonadventure had been a heart attack waiting to happen. But he had to agree with Hannah. It was highly likely that neither science nor good detective skills were going to solve Afoniki's death, no matter how much political pressure was applied.

He pulled his car around behind Sarah's house and parked in the small courtyard next to her catering van and then sat there, wondering how he could reassure Sarah about Bonadventure without betraying his sister's confidence. He gave a frustrated sigh. He really just wanted to see her, to make sure she was okay. It had been hard to drive away last night, but his excuse about not leaving her by herself was no longer valid. Nell and Alex were back in residence.

He blew out an exasperated breath and reached for his keys. This was a bad idea. But before he could restart the car, the door opened and Sarah came out carrying a trash bag, stopping in surprise at the sight of him.

He extracted the keys and clambered out, trying to act like he hadn't been planning to leave.

"Hope you don't mind me parking here," he said.

"It is in the same time zone as my house, unlike anything you could find on St. Charles at this time of day," she said, humor in her voice and questions in her eyes.

"If you're busy, I can—" He gestured back toward his car.

She held up a trash bag. "I don't call this busy."

He strode forward and took it from her, spied the can, went and dumped it, then turned to face her.

"Thank you," she said.

"You're welcome," he said.

The sound of traffic one street over filled what would have otherwise been silence.

"You want to come in?" Sarah said, finally.

"Sure," he said, moving to open the door for her and then following her inside. He wasn't fourteen, he reminded himself. It didn't help. It got easier in the kitchen. Something was giving off really good smells from the stove. He tried not to look at it hopefully.

"Some gumbo?" she added, "I was just about to sit down and have some myself."

He grinned and the tension inside eased. "I'd love some gumbo."

He watched her moving around, securing bowls and utensils. She pulled out his favorite soft drink and handed it to him. There was a homey briskness about her that awakened echoes of Helen, Zach's second wife who was also their not-even-slightly-evil stepmother. And even more distant memories of his mom. This was what he missed, he realized. This was what he'd never had with his ex. She'd never been able to deliver this mix of competence, comfort, and sexy.

Sarah was definitely sexy in her jeans and tee shirt. The way her clothes fit her body and moved with her, the grace in all her movements. All of it called to him in a way that was new. He'd loved his ex, he must have loved her when they got married. He remembered being happy. But what he'd felt for her? He'd lost the memories with the feelings.

Outside the wind began to rattle the windows as an afternoon storm moved in. He looked up, as if he could see through the ceiling to the sky outside.

"Going to rain."

Sarah paused, bowls in each hand and angled her head to listen. "I think you're right. Wish it would clear out the mugginess, but it won't." She slid his bowl across to him, retrieved the bowls of rice and then hooked a foot over the stool closest to her so she could sit down.

"No," he agreed, inhaling the fragrant steam that rose to his face. He tipped in his rice on top, gave it a stir, then dug in and muttered "Dang, that's good."

Her smile rewarded his grunt. Yes, it had been a grunt. He knew better. Good thing Zach wasn't there to pop him on the back of his head.

"Gumbos are tricky. Everyone has their own favorite flavor profile," she said. "A traditional way of making it." She looked up and met his gaze. "No, my mother didn't make gumbo. I learned from her mom."

Mother. Mom. Had he ever heard her call her mother mom? He didn't think so. Not that he had a lot of hours racked up with Sarah. Two days, give or take.

"And then I refined it," Sarah added. "I think Grandma would have approved."

"She would have," Cal said with decision. "This is really good." The words felt lame, but her smile chased the shadows from her eyes. He hadn't realized the shadows were there until they left. The cool blue of her eyes seemed more intense with the red she'd added to her hair. His breath hitched and his heart slammed against his chest.

They ate in silence for a few minutes, then Sarah set her spoon down. "Cinzia stopped by again this morning."

Now his heart jerked. "She did. Why this time?"

"Questions about Basile."

"Any of the others?"

"Not yet. She said he asked her for a job."

Something was bothering her, more than the visit from the wisegal. "What?" he asked, then winced internally at the bluntness of the question.

Her gaze met his, worry clouding the blue. She started to shake her head.

"Tell me," he said, his tone softer this time.

She hesitated for a moment longer, but he kept his gaze on her. "She said she'd been here—in this house—when my parents were alive."

He considered this. "You're worried they were involved with her in some way?"

She nodded.

It was a fair worry but… "They're gone. Does it matter now?" He asked the question knowing it had mattered to Nell, but this was different, wasn't it?

"I can't see how," her lips twisted wryly, "but I keep thinking about Nell. It mattered for her."

So Nell's family problems were fueling this worry. "She has relatives. You don't?"

She shook her head. "Not that I know of, but—" she

bit her lip. "My parents didn't—they weren't good at secrets. It was all pretty much out there."

His hand covered hers before he realized he meant to. "No one thinks you're like them. No one," he added firmly.

"That's what Nell says. And Maisie." A faint smile trembled on her lips.

"Maisie?" Had she mentioned her before?

"You met her last week," Sarah said. "She arrived right after Claude."

"Oh, right." The scene came back to him. The really old lady with the scary gaze. "She's better than my dad with the 'get lost' looks, though don't tell him I said that."

Sarah laughed.

"So who is she?" Cal asked, curious now as memories of the meeting came back to him.

"She's the, well, she's a powerhouse in, you know, the people who go to the fundraisers. The people my parents used to socialize with. You'd like her."

He doubted that. Socially connected little old ladies weren't his thing.

"You would," she insisted, as if he'd said the words out loud. "And you did say you could love her," she reminded him with an impish grin. Then she added, "She's of them without being one of them."

"Okay." Agreement seemed the quickest way to end the discussion.

"I know what you're thinking, but you're wrong. She's one of them because she's rich and she tries to do good, not because she cares what they think." Her brow wrinkled. "She…uses them and their weaknesses to do… good." The cute wrinkles turned into a frown. "She won't like it if someone killed Basile at her fundraiser."

"No one knows if Basile was murdered," Cal pointed out, wishing the conversation hadn't gone here.

"They sure acted like he had been last night," Sarah pointed out. "You…they don't think the two cases are related, do they?"

"I wouldn't think so," Cal said. "Afoniki was stabbed."

"That's true." She stirred the remains of her gumbo with her spoon.

"Are you working tonight?" he asked.

She looked up, startled. "No, thank goodness. I've not got a booking for a couple of weeks, though I do have a petit four order for middle of the week, but that's just a delivery."

"How about a drive, then dinner somewhere?" He was surprised how easily the words came after all his worry, even more surprised by how right it felt to ask.

Her smile came again, sweeping across her face like the sunrise. "I'd like that. Do I need to change?"

"Only if I do, too."

"Let me get my purse," she said. "It won't take me long…"

"I'm not going anywhere," Cal said and realized he meant it.

Chapter Ten

THEY WERE BACK to being easy together, to Sarah's relief. The drive—to nowhere isolated—was followed by dinner at a small "local secret" place in the Irish Channel. She sat back with a happy sigh.

"That was good. Thank you." Just what she'd needed. She kept her gaze down as her insides trembled. Did she need Cal? Because she wasn't sure that was a good idea. All the Baker boys were a bit skittish about commitment. On the one hand, it seemed odd given their dad had committed to two women and was about to commit to a third. But it was possible that losing two moms had given them abandonment issues—issues compounded for Cal with the breakup of his marriage. She didn't know the ins and outs of that—and was not well positioned at the moment to try to find out, since Cal's family all thought she was a double "other woman." Or something.

"You're welcome."

She thought she might have her expression under control enough to look up and smile. The smile trembled at the edges when her gaze met his. Dang, the boy was cute. She'd never been attracted to bad boys. She rooted for the heroes and cheered at the defeat of bad guys. It was probably some complicated Freudian thing because of her parents, who clearly hadn't met a bad guy or girl they didn't invite home.

She envied every single Baker, who had grown up poor and loved and decent. They all worked hard and fought the good fight every day. If they didn't have an "S" hiding on their chests under their clothes, then they deserved to.

And it showed, even in the dim lighting. He was fine and strong and cleanly built. The lines in his face had been earned from living his life as best he could. So of course, her brain called up the image of him in his SWAT gear. Because her heart wasn't beating hard enough.

She glanced around, because she needed to look away before she melted into a puddle—or went up in flames. "Nice place." New Orleans had a lot of places like this. Holes in corners, but they all had great food. A restaurant didn't survive in this city without good food—except maybe in the French Quarter where the tourists kept them going.

"I came here with Decaf—a team member—a few weeks ago," Cal said. "Recognized the neighborhood and remembered it was close by. Glad you like it. You're a tough critic."

"I'm not, actually," Sarah protested, blinking a bit about Decaf. Guys and their nicknames baffled her. "I mean, I know if a place sucks, but when I'm off duty, I'm off duty. And I enjoy having someone else doing the work." She grinned at him and willed her gaze not to cling and her heart not to melt at his answering grin. She was helped by a stirring in the entrance and glanced there, shocked to see Maisie and Valentin entering. She knew Maisie wasn't a snob, but still…this was kind of…slumming.

She didn't look out of place because she didn't dress like a rich old lady, but Valentin was a bit too spiffy, even though his expression suited his surroundings. But then that was his stock-in-trade. She glanced at Cal and saw a bit of revulsion in his eyes at the sight of Valentin. Guys always seemed to be able to tell. At least the alpha ones. She bit her lip at his quickly veiled horror as the elderly couple headed their direction. Cal definitely knew how to do a neutral expression. All those siblings had probably been great training in that.

She rose, cued by Maisie's outstretched arms, and accepted the brisk, powdery hug. It seemed she'd graduated to a higher level in Maisie's queue of people.

Sarah knew not to cling, and when she'd emerged, she studied the old lady with a bit of worry. "Are you all right?" she asked.

"I'm ninety-three," Maisie said with composure as she turned to Cal. "I'd like to introduce you to my friend, Valentin Laurent. Valentin, this is Calvin Baker."

"Baker?" His tone was cultured, as was the discreet rise of his brows.

"Zach Baker's boy," Maisie said.

Sarah gave Cal a discreet glance, half expecting him to shuffle his feet at this reduction to childhood. His lips did twitch as he shook hands with the...escort.

Maisie's gaze met Cal's and Sarah thought she detected a hint of her *look*.

"Any news on Basile Bonadventure's passing?"

Cal shook his head. "No, ma'am."

"He had a heart attack," she said, with enough certainty that Sarah blinked.

Cal made a noncommittal sound and changed the subject. "Have you eaten here before? We were discussing dessert."

Sarah blinked again. Nice diversion, but why did he need or want it?

Maisie made the transition easily enough, recommending the bread pudding. She leaned in with a mischievous look. "We only have an appetizer so we can have dessert."

After a few more exchanges, they moved on to their table and the waiting hostess. She didn't look upset, so they must be used to Maisie. Seated again, Sarah studied Cal, but couldn't find a way to ask him what she wanted to know. It was pure curiosity. Not even a twinge of the sentimental. Death had not altered her distaste for Basile. She might have given an internal sigh, but luckily the bread pudding came. It was as excellent as advertised. When all else failed, there was always dessert.

THE SILENCE WAS comfortable again on the drive back to Sarah's house. He knew she had questions about Basile's death and was grateful she didn't ask them. And he might be a bit impressed. His sisters never held back like that.

He pulled around to the back and parked next to Alex's truck. Lucky Alex who got to stay, who got to climb the stairs with Nell…

Better not to go where he couldn't, or it could get embarrassing. He climbed out and went around to open Sarah's door, extending a hand to help her out. Touching her might have been a mistake. It felt like everything slowed for several seconds. His thoughts. His heart rate. His vision narrowed so that all he saw was her hand in his.

He might be in trouble here, though it was a trouble he couldn't seem to mind.

He lifted his gaze until it met hers and saw a different question in there. It felt like it took forever for his head to bend toward hers. An eternity until his mouth closed over hers. The slow thump of his heart marked the seconds it took for his arms to close around her and pull her close, but it felt like months or even years until she was there. Against his heart and then in it. His heart swelled and started to thump harder, pumping a healing heat into his body.

Healing. He hadn't realized how broken he'd been by the failure of his marriage. Or how much better it could be on the other side. Everything felt better, felt more right. She was soft, responsive, welcoming.

I love you.

It was just as well he couldn't talk while kissing her because it was too soon for the words. Why would she believe him? All he'd done was watch and wish—yes, he had wished, he admitted now—and then he'd kept away from her.

He wouldn't make that mistake again.

When he was sure he could hold back the words, he lifted his head. His hand trembled some when he lifted it to push a strand of hair back behind her ear. Fire sparked in the strands where the streetlamp light got caught there. His other arm tightened around her for several seconds, until he got that control back, too.

"Can we do this again?" he asked. *And again and again?*

The lips he'd just kissed curved upwards in a smile so tender his heart clenched in a mixture of pain and pleasure.

She nodded. "I'd…like that."

The tiny break in her voice made him tremble with the realization of the power he had to hurt her—and for her to hurt him. For a second, he wanted to retreat again, but now, with both arms around her once more, he steadied. He couldn't, he wouldn't. If it broke—but he wouldn't break it this time. And he knew—he didn't know how—that Sarah wasn't the kind to break things.

"I have a heavy work week," he said with regret for the first time about that. "Nights. Can I call or text you?"

She nodded again.

"We could meet for lunch."

"We could. Here or wherever." She lifted a hand, a bit tentatively, and touched his cheek.

He turned his head so that his lips skimmed the skin of her palm. He felt her tremble and tightened his hold, trying to tell her without words that he knew, that he understood, but he was in it to stay. He even wanted to have the "where is this relationship going" talk. He must have smiled, because she smiled, too.

And then, with clear reluctance, she eased out of his hold.

"Good night."

He caught her hand and raised it to his mouth. "Good night."

Letting her go might have been the hardest thing he'd done and he'd done some crazy-crap hard stuff to join SWAT. It wasn't going to be forever, he vowed as she shut the door between them. He'd earn the right to follow her inside and up those stairs.

For a moment his brain balked at the idea of him living in that house, but he didn't have to imagine that, he realized. All he had to do was imagine living with *Sarah*. He could do that.

He saw the light go on in the kitchen and wished he could stay until the trail of lights made it all the way to her bedroom, but he had to go to work. Which was probably a good thing, because for the first time in his life, he kind of understood how a guy could serenade under a woman's bedroom window.

He did not want to go there outside a house where his

big brother lived. With a slight shudder, he turned away, but before he turned onto the street, he looked back. There was a light upstairs. With a quick glance around, he blew a kiss her direction and then resolutely turned his thoughts to work.

Chapter Eleven

"YOU'RE AWFULLY CHEERFUL THESE DAYS," Nell observed from her stool pulled up to the kitchen island.

She and Alex had just exchanged an enthusiastic goodbye and for the first time in a long time, the sight hadn't given Sarah a pang of envy. As far as she knew, none of the Bakers knew how much she and Cal were seeing each other, so this time it was a pang of guilt, since Sarah also hadn't told Nell what was going on. She'd have to come clean, but—and this was the truth—Sarah was afraid to say it out loud. Once the words were out there, anything could happen. Such as them breaking up, and she couldn't endure the thought of all those Baker glances and looks.

But over the past two weeks, she'd felt an increasing confidence in Cal and in them as a couple. Was she deluding herself? Stars in the eyes did obscure the view. She'd observed it in others and experienced it on a smaller level in the past. She'd never felt like this before.

She could admit it to herself. She had…hopes, maybe even some dreams. She hadn't taken to writing Mrs. Calvin Baker on anything but she'd come close a couple of times. It was so high-school, but she felt a bit dreamy and first love-ish. She wanted to plan a wedding—small, well, as small as anything could be with the Bakers involved—and she really, really wanted to plan a honeymoon. Nothing "destination," just a place where they could be alone. She loved being alone with Cal. And she loved the idea of being alone with all the defenses down, all the pretense gone. Alone with the man she loved—there she'd thought it—and with the man who loved her.

Did Cal love her? When she was with him she was certain he did. It was only when they were apart that the doubts crept in.

"Earth to Sarah," Nell's amused voice broke into her thoughts.

Sarah jerked to attention, realizing too late that her smile might have been goofy.

"Sorry," Sarah said, feeling her cheeks heat. "It's a big event tonight." Another one with the same crowd as her last two fun events. Hopefully tonight would not be third time's the bad juju.

Nell sobered immediately. "Are you nervous?"

They both knew it was not like her to be this kind of nervous.

"I might have a bit of PTSD," Sarah admitted. The results of Basile's autopsy had come back negative. He'd died of a heart attack. He hadn't been murdered. There'd been no sign of wiseguy or gal interest in her for two weeks now. Two happy weeks, she reminded herself. "I wish tonight was a different crowd."

"I don't blame you," Nell said. "Do you want me to come along and help out?"

Hold her hand is what she meant. Alex was on night shift so she'd planned to work on her book, Sarah knew. She hesitated, but this was the time to adult. She couldn't panic before every event. And this "crowd" was a lucrative source of future income. It was a step up and that could become a step back if Sarah didn't adult this.

"I'll be fine," Sarah said. "According to Zach, it's better to get back on the horse."

"Says the man who has never ridden a horse in his life," Nell pointed out, but with a grin and possibly a hint of relief. Nell was on deadline.

"At least this one doesn't have an ice sculpture," Sarah said, with an answering grin. "And I'll make sure we keep control of the knives."

Nell's face relaxed some more. "If you're sure…"

"I am sure," Sarah said, and felt her insides quiver as if she'd challenged the universe now. Well, the universe had delivered some smackdowns and she was still standing. Though she wasn't stupid enough to think "bring it." You couldn't grow up in New Orleans without being a little superstitious. Maybe she should have put some *gris gris* on the voodoo queen's grave. Well, it was too late now to hedge her bets. She straightened her shoulders and put on her brave face.

"Once more into the fray—" She didn't finish the quote. Saying or thinking it was her last good fight was not a good idea either. She was not going to live or die on a dinner.

She hoped.

———

THERE'D BEEN some rumblings in the dark underbelly of the city, a sense of something about to happen, so Cal's team was on duty. Not beat patrolling, but as the QRT—the quick response team—which meant they were geared up and ready to deploy. Those in charge had learned the hard way not to ignore the rumblings. And they'd been expecting something to happen after Afoniki's murder. The power balance between the three mob families was always tenuous at best. The arrival of an Afoniki heir had heightened, not lessened, tensions according to Frank.

Cal just wished he could put to rest his concern that all of this could reach out to touch Sarah. It hadn't even been her piece of ice, but it bothered him they'd all showed up to talk to her. And it bothered him even more that there just didn't seem to be a way out to solve it, to ever find Afoniki's killer.

But the part of the city that Cal knew the best was tense—strung wire-taut. And that tension was reflected in the faces of his fellow team members. Even their commander, Big Chip, looked grimmer than usual, though BuzzKill was playing a game on his cellphone. BuzzKill never got tense until he had to.

Decaf had his eyes closed, probably trying to Zen his

way through the night—which they'd all be repeating for
as many nights as it took to cool things down.

Minion, their new guy, was trying to look cool, but the
jiggle of his knee gave him away. Pluto? He was his own
planet—and still believed the planet should be, too.

Takeaway was eating some fast food he'd managed to
pick up somehow. FunSize sat like the big, solid rock he
was, eclipsing Eclipse seated next to him.

Cal dealt with his inner tension by running code
strings through his head, one finger absently tapping the
butt of his lowered weapon. He looked up and found
FunSize staring at him.

"What?" Cal asked.

"Something's different," FunSize said.

Cal was grateful the light in their van wasn't that
good, as color heated his cheeks. He arched his brows. He
had learned the art of the bluff at his brothers' knees.

FunSize lifted his fingers, pointing two at Cal and
then two at his eyes in the universal "I'm watching you"
gesture.

Cal almost said something, because the words wanted
to bust out, but he had a feeling he should tell Sarah
before FunSize.

"Bite me," he told FunSize, and everyone laughed,
even Big Chip. For a moment the tension lightened.

IT DIDN'T HELP that thunder rumbled in the distance
halfway through the unloading of the van. Great.

It was a dark and stormy night.

She almost tensed, waiting for that shot to ring out. In New Orleans at night? More than one shot was likely to ring out.

She and her staff picked up the pace, anxious to have everything inside before the rain started. And then she forgot her worries in the familiar process of getting everything set up. It felt like they were all back to normal. The staff was on top of everything, the guests were grabbing the food almost as fast as they could get it down. The music was jazz and the AC was keeping up with the crowd.

It was almost as if everyone—guests in particular—were trying to shake off the shadows from both previous events. The chatter was animated and even the snootiest were sporting smiles. Not one of her old friends snubbed her.

Maybe they thought they'd die, she thought, able to be amused finally. Dark humor, but at least her sense of humor was coming back. Though she didn't share this or any ice-sculpture jokes with anyone. She could save them for Cal. She kept the smile under cover, but it warmed her up. Another date tomorrow night. Yeah, she was going to have to confess all to Nell. She was kind of surprised no one had seen them. The Baker coverage of New Orleans was pretty extensive. But they'd stuck to small places with dark corners. And so far, Maisie hadn't talked. The old lady knew how to keep a secret.

Speaking of…Sarah studied the crowd and found her and Valentin off to the side. They'd staked out one of the small tables and were holding court there. She still looked like Miss Marple had wandered into the wrong party, but Valentin had his dashing on.

Sarah turned back to her tables, running an expert eye down the line, then headed for the kitchen to make sure her ducks were still lined up in the right rows.

The mood in the kitchen was cheerful. They were on the downside of the evening and there had been no glitches and no deaths. Score. It was time to roll out the sweets. The trays looked so inviting, Sarah had to resist the urge to bury her face in one of them.

"Let's—" she began, but the words were cut off by a single shot and then the sound of breaking glass.

"Out!" she ordered, gesturing toward the back door. "Now!" Mentally she counted as she backed toward the door to the main ballroom. She had two more—before she reached the door they ran in, followed by several guests. She gestured to them to keep running as she grabbed her purse and extracted her cellphone and keys. She tossed her van keys to the last staffer.

"Sarah—" she protested.

"I'll be right behind you," Sarah said. She had to make sure all her people were out. The girl ran out and Sarah reached out to ease the door open, but it was yanked open before her hand touched it.

The man holding the gun was one of the Afoniki's bodyguards. Her first thought was, *When did they get out of jail?* And her second—*They'd found the kitchen this time.*

Chapter Twelve

THE MOOD in the van changed to serious as soon as the call came in. There was a lurch as they turned. Big Chip's face was serious, and got edged with grim, as he listened to the details. Finally he lowered his cellphone, his gaze moving around the team before finally stopping on Cal. It seemed like he hesitated.

"We've got a report of shots fired at another charity thing," he said. He gave the address, but Cal already knew it. "First guys on the scene are reporting quiet but place is locked down."

Sarah. Tension rippled down his back and settled in his gut.

"You gonna be okay, Ghost?" Big Chip asked, his gaze dispassionate and grim.

"I'm fine," he said shortly. "What do we know?"

"We got command on the way but we're gonna be first on scene after the beat cop." He hesitated then added, "Some guests managed to get out and they're saying it's the same guys from last time, Afoniki's bodyguards."

That made no sense. None. He didn't ask why they were out of jail. Someone had bailed them and then— this? What the—

"Since we're first on scene, it's our job to find out as much as we can," Big Chip said. "We're lucky it's a public-event business. Most of the layout of the building is online. Sending it to your phones to memorize."

There was a ping as it arrived. Cal studied the series of images, noting exits and entrances. These wouldn't give them vents or other access. They'd have to find those as they moved in.

"One minute out. Check your gear again."

Cal bent and began his check, the process of prepping —both physically and mentally—helped, as Big Chip knew it would.

"Any fatalities that we know of?" Cal asked, even as his hands moved from pocket to pocket.

"No."

Sarah. He'd been so worried that he'd die on the job, he hadn't thought about that flip side. What if—he tamped the thought down. He had to focus. If she was still alive—*No, don't think that either.* She was alive and she needed him. She needed his training; she needed him to do his job.

AT LEAST THIS time they hadn't made Sarah sit down with her hands clasped behind her back. Yet. She had a feeling that was coming, since all the guests and musicians who hadn't managed to escape were contained in the center of the floor with their hands clasped behind their heads.

It pained Sarah to see Maisie and her elderly gigolo, Valentin in the group. They were too old for this crap, though both managed to retain their dignity somehow. Valentin managed to retain his look of majestic unconcern.

Sarah glanced around as she was tugged, somewhat politely, toward the other three former bodyguards. She wasn't thrilled about the thug's grip on her upper arm, but she was relieved there were no dead bodies, at least that she could see.

The three thugs stood in a line covering the seated guests. They weren't having any crowd-control problems. The guests, for the most part, looked shell-shocked.

When they'd reached a position somewhat center of the gathering, the thug pulled her to a stop and gestured toward the crowd.

"Who did it?" he said.

"Who did what?" Sarah prompted.

"Killed Mr. Afoniki," he answered with some impatience. "We will not go to jail for crime we did not commit." His Russian accent was heavier as his agitation grew.

Sarah blinked, trying to process this.

"If paid, this different, jail time included," he added.

The three others nodded solemnly. "But this is not pay, this frame, and we hear trouble for us from Mr. Pavel."

She must have made a face, because he asked, "You know Mr. Pavel?"

"I met him briefly." She couldn't stop the follow-up grimace.

"You no like him?" He sounded surprised. "He like you."

"How…nice," she said without enthusiasm. And they had wandered off topic a bit. "Look…"

"We not kill Mr. Afoniki," he insisted.

Sarah knew there were worries of some kind of a war breaking out between the crime families. She stole a quick look around. This was not that.

She studied her captor, even more closely than the last time. He was big, broad, tough looking, and yes, she sensed he was scared. Or worried.

"I, um, sort of thought you were, um, in jail," Sarah said, stalling for time. Her brain felt sluggish and the whole of her body was ice. Like she was the ice sculpture this time.

The main thug did not look offended, though his brows drew together in a fierce frown.

"We released on bail," he said. "We know what this means."

"That you're not in jail?" she suggested even knowing she should probably not talk. Was this what shock did? She knew on the other side of the ice that terror lived there and possibly panic. She couldn't afford to panic. Even in a shocked stupor, her brain cataloged signs of stress and tension in all four men. They were tinder waiting for the match and they had nothing to lose.

"We are marked men." He half shrugged. "Not that we were any safer inside. Is tough business."

"I can…imagine." Thanks to television she thought she could, anyway.

"You will help us or peoples will die," he said, gesturing over his shoulder. He blinked rapidly.

She tried to smile, not sure she had managed it.

"Neither of us wants that." Did he? She knew she didn't, but was she speaking for him? She knew the thought was weird, possibly trivial, but she was working to quell her own panic. Was it PTSD or *deja vu* when she was back where it started? She had to focus. "You know I'm not any kind of sleuth, don't you?"

"You are clever, observant. You cook good."

Right. Well, she could see how she could get confused with a sleuth on those grounds.

"Plus you live with cop."

"I don't live with—he's married to my roommate. Different floors, even." She moved her hands so that one was above the other. "Completely different—anyway—" she was getting lost in the weeds. "Most of my deductive skills come from watching television, which means it's all fake."

"You do it or they will die," he said, with more force than the last time. And he waved his gun for emphasis.

She looked at the seated group and saw fear, lots of fear, with Maisie the only calm one. Could she help?

She bit her lip and turned back to the thug, "Look—I'm sorry, I don't know your name?"

"Vlad."

Of course it was. "Look Vlad, may I call you Vlad?" He nodded sharply. "You know what everyone thinks, right?"

"I do. But they are wrong."

"Logically, it just makes sense that one of you—" she swallowed when his gaze narrowed. "It makes sense that one of them," she said, nodding toward the other three, "did it. Those people aren't skilled enough and they don't have a motive."

"Motive can be many things," he said.

"Yeah, but let's face it. The big ones are money and power. Who stood to benefit?"

"Pavel Afoniki," he conceded, but his stubborn look deepened. "He hired one of them." He gestured with the gun again.

Sarah looked at the sea of pasty-faced suspects and swallowed. She wanted to protest again, but that wasn't going to go well, if she was reading this guy right. She glanced toward the kitchen and this time he followed her gaze.

"We have locked all doors. Won't surrender until truth is out. Or everyone dead."

"Okay then. I think everyone wants to cooperate, so there's no need to start shooting." Time…Cal and the others needed time, so she'd try to give them time. Somehow. She looked around, then pointed at a table and chairs that were close by. "On…television, they question the, um, suspects. May I?"

He nodded, his gaze suspicious but also showing a bit hope. Good thing someone had some.

She dragged the table over and then got two chairs. No one tried to help her, even though they didn't look that busy guarding that cowed bunch. One glance had told her there were no heroes waiting for their moment. No, all the heroes were outside.

Trying to look official—whatever that was—Sarah sat down and surveyed the suspects.

"Not everyone here was there that night," she said. This bunch was bigger for one thing, despite those that had managed to escape. She was also pretty sure not everyone from the last time was here, but she wasn't going to bring that up.

"They are expendable then," Vlad said.

"If you let them leave, it would be a sign of good faith and would put off—" she stopped.

"SWAT breaking in and shooting us?" Vlad considered this—or appeared to. "We have talked. We do not mind going out in, how you say, blaze of glory. Better than floating facedown in river."

Okay, he was not considering it the way she'd hoped… and would they float? She thought they used concrete…

Focus, Sarah.

"I'll just ask everyone here a few questions then," Sarah said. "I can't really remember who was and wasn't here. I was just moving the canapés."

"Very well." He stepped behind her back and gestured at someone.

With a gasp, an older debutante shrank back against the guy next to her.

"It's…okay," Sarah said. "Just come and sit down. It will rest your tush."

This seemed to help. The guy helped her stand, then hurriedly returned his hands to the back of his neck and his tush to the hard floor. The woman approached with clear reluctance and sat down on the very edge of the chair.

Maybe it would help to humanize them?

"What's your name?" Sarah said, giving her a smile that she hoped didn't look as tense as it felt.

———

BIG CHIP SENT CAL, BuzzKill, Eclipse, Decaf, Pluto, and FunSize to do a circuit of the exterior of the catering company's building, looking for possible egress points further from the main action—and less likely to be heard by the perps. If it was only four guys inside, no way could they secure the whole structure.

Cal found a fire escape and reported it.

After a pause to orient the spot with the interior, Big Chip gave them the go-ahead to enter.

"Alarms?" FunSize paused to ask.

"Owner has verified the system is dormant," Big Chip told them.

Cal and the others stacked on the side of the door

that would open and waited while FunSize used the breacher. In two more seconds they were inside. FunSize reported entry and then followed them in.

They were in a dimly lit office area with both sides leading off to cubicles. If the map they'd seen was correct, the party rental suites were straight ahead. Cal switched on his night sight as he took his turn clearing each cubicle before moving forward. They reached a locked door. They were more central in the building, so FunSize was extra careful with the breach.

They were also more cautious entering this corridor. It was wider and carpeted, with chairs and vases dotted along its length. A public area. To their left was the top of a wide staircase. They approached this with extra care and Cal took a quick look over the railing.

It was a foyer. More carpet and fancier decor, if he was any judge, which he wasn't. They used hand signals now. FunSize waited at the top to cover the others as they padded quietly down the curved stairs. They stacked against a wall and Cal peered around. Bingo.

This was it. Out a bank of glass doors he could see their van and a huddle of cop cars with flashing lights making tracks across the otherwise unlit space.

Cal signaled for the others to hold and eased forward, padding silently toward one of two sets of doors into the main ballroom. No windows in either set of doors. He might have cussed silently.

He backtracked and activated his radio.

He gave his location. "Permission to deploy my eyes."

"Hold," Big Chip said. "We're looking for a vent up top to give us a bird's eye."

Cal might have rolled his eyes. Those doors weren't heavy. They could be inside and toss a couple of FNDs, but that might be bad PR. It wasn't good to use flash bangs and make victims wet their pants.

"Ghost?" Big Chip's voice was sharp.

"Roger that."

THE BAD GUYS were getting restless and increasingly unimpressed with Sarah's interrogation skills. One recommended a more forceful questioning technique. Sarah turned to look at him, trying to make as much human contact as was possible.

"People who are…forcefully questioned will say what you want, particularly people not trained to be questioned that way," Sarah pointed out. She glanced back at the anxious middle-aged man occupying her hot seat. "If you finger the wrong person, you won't gain anything."

"We will no longer be under suspicion," a younger thug pointed out.

"Won't you? Won't…the people perhaps targeting you be…diverted when it makes no sense?" Sarah took a deep breath and rose, facing Vlad. "Everyone thinks you, one of you, did it. You know it. I know it. A…sham investigation won't change that."

"The person who killed Mr. Afoniki is in this room," Vlad insisted.

"Yes," she agreed. They were in this room, too.

As if he heard this thought, his mouth twisted.

"None of us did it."

She arched a brow, but kept sympathy in her gaze.

"We are brothers," his voice was low. "Brothers in action and by birth. We are blood."

Sarah did not have a lot of personal trust in blood ties, but she knew Cal and his brothers trusted theirs. So it was possible that bad-guy brothers had a form of trust.

She had no idea if she could figure this out, but stalling wasn't working anymore. They needed a sense she was seriously trying to help them or the shooting would start. She bit her lower lip and looked around, hoping for some inspiration and then—maybe—she saw it.

"Miss Maisie," she murmured. If anyone knew of any shady connections, Sarah bet she would. Sadly, she was betting on this with all their lives.

"What?" he asked sharply.

"Miss Maisie Daigle. She might, could…help. She knew everyone here. This is her party." Sarah felt a bit like a traitor, outing her to the bad guys, but the old lady was tough. And it would get her off the floor and into a chair. "She's your best hope."

Vlad stared at her for a long time, her heart thudding out the seconds.

"No stall?"

She shook her head. "No stall. Best hope," she repeated.

Finally he nodded, giving permission with a jerk of his weapon.

Sarah stepped through the seated people, trying to look reassuring. In front of Miss Maisie, she stopped and crouched.

"I need your help, ma'am," she said. "This is going to go south fast if they don't believe we're really trying to find out who killed Afoniki."

"What do you need me to do?" she asked, calmly.

Sarah rose and held out her hand. Valentin tried to get up to help, too, but he was too stiff and Maisie put a hand on his knee.

"No, Valentin, I can do this." She took Sarah's hand.

The old lady wasn't that heavy. Most of the weight was probably in her purse that came up with her. Sarah feared she'd snap the frail bones of her hands. Her wrist was a bird-leg thing, though Sarah also recalled the strength in the claw-like grip. She was tougher than she looked. Maisie swayed for a moment, an indication of how hard the long time on the floor had been for her. Sarah slipped a hand around her waist.

"Come sit down, ma'am," she said.

The seated figures moved aside for them and Sarah didn't think it was her imagination that a wave of hope followed them. Maisie was the bomb, no question.

When Sarah had helped her sit in the chair she herself had been occupying, she moved to the chair facing her and sat, trying not to think about it being the hot seat. She cast a look at Vlad, who had moved into a position between them. She half expected him to object to the purse. He did give Maisie a threatening look and then

stepped back, half startled. Sarah caught the tail end of
Maisie's look and flinched.

Dang, the old lady was good.

"Ma'am, Vlad here," she said, indicating the thug,
"believes he and his…team have been unfairly suspected.
He…they believe Afoniki's killer is in this room and I'm
hoping that you can help us narrow down the suspects.
Will you help us?"

Sarah knew she was stalling with the questions.
Things had to be happening outside. She had to give
them time. More than anything, she wanted to see Cal
and his team burst in.

"Of course," the old lady said, composedly. "But,"
she said, directing her formidable gaze in Vlad's direction
once again, "you need to release the innocent. You know
not all of these people were here last time."

Vlad opened his mouth, perhaps to tell Maisie what
he'd told Sarah—that they'd make good victims—but he
closed it again and, after a pause, he nodded.

"How do I know you won't let killer leave?" Vlad
asked, though without much force.

"You have my word," she said, composedly.

He nodded again, a sort of reluctant respect in his
gaze.

"Can I call and let them know outside that some
people are coming out?" Sarah asked. It would really suck
if the good guys shot them.

He reached for his cellphone, but Sarah, pulled out
hers and held it up. Vlad took it, verified that it was not
recording them and handed it back.

Sarah looked at it, hesitating.

"What's wrong, dear?"

"Should I call nine-one-one?"

"That will take too long," Maisie said. "Call Nell and ask her to have someone call you."

Sarah looked at Vlad and he nodded again. Maybe he really was trying to clear his name.

"Put on speaker," Vlad directed, as she started to dial.

Now it was Sarah's turn to nod.

The phone was answered on the first ring and Nell's voice seemed to echo around the room.

"Sarah! Are you all right?"

"I need you to help me out, Nell. Can you get my number to someone in command outside?"

"Then it's true—"

"You're on speaker, Nell. Can you help me out?"

A silence.

"Of course." A pause. "Love you, Sarah."

"Love you, Nell." Sarah pushed the button to cut the connection and then set the phone on the table. "It shouldn't take long," Sarah said, with a large measure of hope that she was right.

"While we wait, let's separate out those who aren't involved in this, shall we?" Maisie said.

Vlad gave her another searching look and then stood back in much permission. The other three exchanged looks, but didn't speak. Maybe Maisie's look had gotten to them, too.

CAL SHIFTED from one foot to the other. They'd checked out all the rooms on the ground floor and were now back watching the doors of the main ballroom. The waiting was the hardest part. He had a new kind of appreciation for this kind of waiting, the kind when you had someone inside…

"Big Chip," he murmured into his radio. "SitRep?"

"We've got another team inside—" he broke off, and then, after a pause said sharply, "Hold. We've got intel they are letting some people go."

Cal signaled to the team and they moved deeper into the shadow of the ladies' room. He hoped no one needed to use it…

———

THE GROUP HAD MOSTLY BEEN DIVIDED when the call came through. Sarah sought visual permission from Vlad before answering—on speaker.

"Miss Burland?"

Sarah didn't recognize the voice, but the fact that he knew her name—and called her "miss"—gave her hope she hadn't got a spam call at the wrong time.

"Yes." She had to clear the huskiness, or perhaps it was fear, from her throat. "This is Sarah Burland."

"We're happy to hear from you, ma'am," the calm voice said. It was deep and soothing, but it wasn't Cal. Of course it wasn't Cal. No one knew she was dating Cal. And he was probably deployed somewhere waiting to bust in. No time to chat. "Can you give us some insight into your situation?"

Sarah got another sharp nod from Vlad, but also a warning look.

"Some people are going to come out. It would be nice if you didn't shoot them," she said.

Vlad's nod this time was approving.

"What—" The voice began.

Vlad reached down and closed the connection.

"That is enough."

Some signal passed between the four men, then one of them began to herd the lucky ones toward the doorway. He produced some keys and they shuffled out of sight.

Sarah couldn't look at the ones still waiting. Maisie had accomplished what Sarah couldn't, but now what?

———

LIGHT from the ballroom doors changed the pattern of lights in the foyer and there was a murmur, a very low murmur of voices accompanied by the sounds of shuffling movement.

Cal was flattened against the wall, but he risked a look when the sound grew louder. About twenty people had reached one bank of outer doors, stopped as someone worked on the lock. He couldn't see Sarah in the huddle. Didn't mean she wasn't there, even though his gut told him she wasn't.

The ballroom door swung closed and there was the

closer sound of a key being used. It would have been a bad time to act anyway. The perps would have been on high alert with the door open.

Whoever was using the key on the outside door was pushed back by someone, then the door finally opened and the huddle of people tried to push through the opening all at once. Some cops ran forward and began to sort—and cover them—urging them toward the safety of the police cars. One of them tried to turn and lock the door, but the cops half dragged her away protesting.

Cal and the team waited to see how the perps would react to this—or if they'd bothered to watch. That was not a position Cal would have liked. Big Chip knew that he and BuzzKill were close and so was a sniper.

"As soon as you're clear, deploy your eyes," Big Chip told him.

Chapter 13

THIS TIME VLAD went and got a chair and dragged it over to the table, then seated himself between Sarah and Miss Maisie. He leaned back in the chair as if he were also glad to be sitting, but his air of alertness had not stood down.

This close, his body gave off a sour, almost acrid smell. It could have been fear, or maybe he hadn't showered after getting bailed out of jail. Or maybe she blamed him for the fear that was actually emanating from the hostages—of which she was one, she reminded herself.

Into this mix of nasty, came a soft powdery floral that had to be Miss Maisie. Her faded gaze was calm, reflective even. She looked at Vlad and finally spoke.

"I need a glass of water, young man." She lifted a thin wrist and studied the tiny, loose-fitting watch. "I have to take my medication."

After a short pause, Vlad signaled to the youngest of his brothers. "Take her to get water for old…lady."

Since he pointed at Sarah, she took this to mean she was to fetch the water, though why the thug couldn't fill a glass…

"I'll be right back," Sarah assured her. She was taken into the kitchen by the thug, so worried by her act of bringing Miss Maisie to the goons' attention, she didn't notice anything off with her current goon until he spoke.

"You are not a bad looking broad," he said, giving her a look that was decidedly lascivious.

"I have a boyfriend," she said, turning back to the sink and filling a glass as quickly as possible. She turned to face him, holding the glass up between them—while planning what to do if he didn't take her back to the ballroom.

Maybe the look in her eyes dissuaded him—she was almost old enough to be his mother—because he turned with a shrug and held the door open for her. Wow, manners of a sort. Sarah made sure they didn't touch as she slipped past—yeah, this one had a stench going on, too.

Back inside the ballroom, Sarah was struck by the tableau-ness of it. The AC had caught up and passed the occupancy. It was cold and somehow stale, though that wasn't the right description either. It was…wrong. It smelled off and ominous. Did ominous smell?

There were the two sinister goons pacing around the huddle of hostages with their weapons pointing at them. The wilted important people were almost too weary to be afraid anymore. They stared at their captors with despair.

And then there was Miss Maisie and Vlad seated at the delicate table, like Miss Marple and whatever cop she was about to astonish with her deductions.

Agatha Christie would have liked the setup. It lent itself to a reveal and a confession—if the suspects hadn't been so wrong. It was as if the show had switched players with a romantic comedy or something.

And Miss Maisie didn't, she couldn't, have a deduction to pull out of her big purse. At best, all she could offer were some insights or suspicions.

Sarah crossed over and set the water down in front of her as the young goon rejoined his brothers on patrol.

Maybe something in his brother's face or the way he moved caught Vlad's attention because he shot him a stern look. The young man hunched a shoulder like a surly teen.

"He was not rude?" Vlad asked Sarah.

Sarah hesitated—was it rude to be told she wasn't bad looking?—and finally shook her head. Much as she'd liked to have sewn the seeds of discord with these guys, she couldn't see how it would help them.

Vlad did not look convinced and sent his brother another stern look.

It was…interesting that Vlad had sort of set himself up as her protector—of sorts. He hadn't ruled out shooting her, she reminded herself.

While these thoughts ran through Sarah's head, Miss Maisie opened her capacious bag and extracted a bottle of pills—not the weapon Sarah might have wistfully wished for. With some fumbling, she managed to open the lid and shake two out into a hand that had a hint of a tremble to it. She placed first one, then the second into her mouth and lifted the glass, sipping delicately once, then twice more.

The skin of her throat was so thin, Sarah would have sworn she saw both pills go down. She set the half-full glass back on the table and folded her hands on the tabletop in an attitude of interrogation.

"Now, where were we?"

Before Vlad could voice a demand, Sarah cut him off. "I'm so sorry for getting you into this, ma'am," Sarah said. "It's just that—"

"You weren't getting very far, were you?" Miss Maisie said, the kindness in her eyes robbing the words of reprimand. "It's an unfortunate situation."

"Yes," Sarah said, a bit bemused. "And sadly, you are the one person here who knows everyone and—" she stopped herself from saying, "where all the bodies are buried."

"You were here also when Bonadventure died," Vlad said, unexpectedly. "Which of these—"

"Basile Bonadventure," Miss Maisie's tone was acidic enough to override Vlad's despite the low tone, "died of a heart attack." That tone might have indicated "and good thing, too." Or perhaps, "and not before his time."

Vlad might have blinked. Sarah knew she did. Cal had told her this but how did Miss Maisie know? Stupid question. She always seemed to know.

"Dimitri Afoniki's death was clumsy, no question, an

impulse of the moment," Miss Maisie said, almost reflectively. "When one gets older, one's impulse control is lessened."

Sarah found her brows pulling in. Was she—Sarah glanced in Valentin's direction and saw a look of such tender sadness on a face that had dealt for years in fake emotion. *Valentin?*

"But it would be most inappropriate to let the innocent—or even the far from innocent be involved," she said, the acid back in her voice.

She was right. It was hard to call any of this lot innocent.

"No one should suffer or pay a price for something they did not do," Miss Maisie said, her voice gentle again.

"Yes, this is why we come," Vlad said.

Maisie's gaze turned in his direction and the wisps of her brows rose.

"Is true," he insisted, though with less force. "We are" —her look turned stern—

"—not guilty of…this crime." His tone had weakened even more.

"While justice might be served by having you… indicted for Afoniki's death, my sense of personal honor would be offended," Miss Maisie admitted. "I was brought up to take responsibility for my own actions."

Sarah glanced at Valentin again. Was this lecture for him? Was she hoping he'd do it, say it himself? He looked so sad, but he just shook his head when he looked at her as if she was the one who didn't understand.

She turned back to Miss Maisie, her thoughts swirling

and unformed. The old lady swayed a bit and grabbed the edge of the table.

"I must have misjudged how long it would take for the pills to take effect," she said. "Age does that to one. Mistakes. It is time to end my work."

Her...work? Sarah swallowed. Her glance at Vlad showed he still hadn't got it—if she had. Because Sarah still didn't believe Miss Maisie...

Sarah reached out and covered the trembling old hands. The ice had taken them over already. Sarah could see...death...creeping across her face.

"You killed him, Miss Maisie?" Sarah said, unable to keep the quiver out of her voice. She sensed, rather than saw Vlad turn sharply, bringing the gun up.

"Wait," she said. "Let her talk. Let her finish."

He hesitated, then nodded. But he didn't lower his weapon.

"I knew no one would know," Miss Maisie went on, as if they hadn't spoken. "It was an impulse, not like the others."

"The...others?" Sarah asked, faintly.

"I tried to show restraint," she said, panting a little between her words now. "Just one a year, though there are so many people who aren't good, aren't there?" She looked at Sarah now and the sweetness was still in her gaze—along with a little crazy and the shadow of death. "It is nice to be able to say it after so long."

How long?

Vlad's gaze, meeting hers, was as startled as Sarah felt.

"I lost him, you know?" she murmured, sagging to one side. "I loved him and they killed him."

"They?" Sarah prompted.

"His so-called friends. They were drunk. It was an accident they said. It was a choice, I told them, and they brushed me off. So I killed them, oh, not right away. Slowly, over the years. Once they were gone I just…kept doing it. I only killed those who weren't nice."

"I'm sure you did, ma'am," Sarah said, sliding her chair over so she could support the beginning-to-sag old woman. It didn't take much effort.

"I killed Dimitri for you, Sarah. He was always bothering you." A trembling hand freed itself from Sarah's clasp and patted her hand. It felt like an ice claw against her skin. "You're a nice young woman, Sarah. You deserved better."

The lids fluttered down and her breathing shallowed. Only then did it occur to Sarah to ask, "What did you take, Miss Maisie?"

But it was too late. There was a series of shallow pants and then it stopped. And suddenly Miss Maisie was a surprising deadweight in Sarah's arms.

Dead weight. Dead.

She looked up and met Vlad's gaze.

"Now you know," she said. What next? "What's your exit plan?" Did they have one?

Vlad was still shocked. Sarah looked at the other hostages. She was pretty sure Valentin was the only one who knew what had happened. Tears tracked slowly down cheeks that sagged now as if from a blow. He must have known, but this didn't seem like a good time to mention that.

Not too eagerly, Sarah's attention returned to Vlad. The shock was beginning to fade, his gaze almost dispassionate as he studied the body Sarah still clutched, awkwardly now that the life had left it.

His gaze rose to meet hers and something in there spread a new level of cold fear through her body.

"You know many police," he said. His gaze studied what of her body he could see. "Perhaps I even let you live if you please."

The chill turned to a sick churn.

"Is safer for you if you cooperate," he added, as if he sensed she was not on board with him.

"Safer?" Sarah's voice was not as calm as she'd have liked. A definite squeak there at the end.

He reached out, his hand massive with thick, square fingers, and took her hand.

"Is better to cooperate," he said.

THE IMAGE from his filament eyes was not as sharp as he'd have liked. Cal adjusted the focus, sharpening it on Sarah and the people at the table with her.

She seemed to be clutching the old lady who looked slumped in her arms. Then the thug reached out and took her hand, bringing his weapon up to the level of her face. The sick look of fear in her eyes reached across the distance. Cal felt his gut clench as instinct took over.

"Something's going down. We need to move now," Cal said. "I'm pretty sure one of the hostages is dead or injured."

"We should—" Big Chip began.

"Trust me, something has changed. It's gonna go south."

The body language of the three thugs standing watch over the other hostages had changed, too.

There was a short pause, then Big Chip said, "Go."

In a smooth movement, the six of them divided into teams of two and stacked near the three double doors. Cal and BuzzKill were on either side of their doors, each with a hand on the handle to pull the door their way.

There was a silent countdown and they yanked the doors open, looking for targets as they ran in. Cal aimed at the thug with Sarah.

As if he had a sixth sense, he turned toward them. The force of Cal's rapid fire slammed him back. He crashed onto the table and slid to the floor.

Cal turned for another target, but the other three were already down. With FunSize and Pluto providing cover, the others approached each downed target and secured their hands and weapons.

Cal kept his sights on the thug by Sarah until he was secured, then finally lowered his weapon and lifted his goggles so he could see Sarah. And she could see him.

She was so pale, she could have been a ghost. She swayed, taking a half step toward him, then stopped, glancing around. But she managed a wisp of a smile.

To heck with this, he thought and strode forward, his

arms reaching out to her. He knew he wasn't good hugging with all his gear, but she didn't seem to mind. He leaned down so that his lips were against her ear.

"I love you, Sarah," he said.

Chapter 14

SARAH HESITATED at the top of the last flight of stairs. It was the morning after and that song from the movie where the ship tipped over kept playing in head. She was fortunate to have a morning after. Her head knew this. Her heart, well, her heart was a tangled mess of shock at what almost happened and mush from Cal's very public hug. And his very private declaration. She'd been too shocked to respond, but she hoped the way she'd clung to him was a partial answer.

She'd been too overwhelmed to say anything. And then, not surprisingly, events had pushed them apart. She'd had to find her voice, had to try to explain why and how Miss Maisie had died. At some point, Cal's sister Hannah had appeared and had been very interested in Sarah's—and Miss Maisie's—story.

She'd kept her gaze away from the tumbled bodies of the former bodyguards while the crime scene was processed. It was challenging to sort through her feelings there. She felt relief because she'd never again have to look up and see one of them pointing a weapon in her face. And she felt…guilt. The logical part of her knew it was unfounded, but it was there. Had she, in some way given Vlad encouragement when she talked them into laying down their guns the first time?

It was a peculiarly female problem. She'd read about it, felt it, fought it. And was fighting it now. Vlad made the choice to invade the party and then there were his threats—she'd seen his eyes. He'd felt no mercy for her or for anyone he'd threatened. As Miss Maisie would have said—Sarah's hands shook where she gripped the railing —they weren't nice men. If Cal and his team hadn't ended the situation—

She pressed her lips together as this new round of PTSD gave her lots of worst-case scenarios to obsess over. Okay, truth time.

She'd rather feel guilty than afraid.

They'd left in handcuffs and come back. The justice system wasn't perfect. Maybe they'd have gone to jail and moved on or gone away when they got out. And maybe they'd have come back. Not because she was so stalk-worthy, but because they were…not nice men.

The efficiency with which Cal and his team had removed the threat, well, she might feel a bit guilty by how much that impressed her. It had all been violent and shocking and—Cal was really good at what he did. He'd been hard to hug in his gear, but hard didn't matter. He felt good, he was good. He was a good man.

I love you.

Part of her was afraid she'd imagined the words he'd breathed into her ear. But she hadn't imagined the very public hug. In front of witnesses, even.

Speaking of…Her house wasn't fully baked, but she'd seen cars arriving and heard the voices in her kitchen. Nell had warned her by text, but she had a feeling the baking had grown since that text. And that would be why she was stuck here at the top of the stairs in her own house.

The cook was getting baked when what she really wanted was kisses from the guy who'd saved her life.

She sank down on the top step and leaned against the banister, peering down into the hall through the slats. How many times in her life had she sat in this spot trying to work up nerve—or avoid—going down and joining some event of her parents? The wood felt cool against her forehead and the curves of the wood were all too familiar. Swept back in the past, she closed her eyes and let herself remember the good and the bad.

For too long the bad had dominated the list, but she'd run down these same steps on Christmas mornings, for birthdays, and first dates. Prom nights and mornings after where they'd sat and talked and laughed. She had laughed with her parents. The divide had grown wider and deeper as she moved into adulthood and seen them with clearer eyes—but her parents had loved her in their way, and as much as they could. They'd had flaws, some big ones, but then so did everyone.

Miss Maisie. For the first time since she'd given her statement, Sarah let herself think about Miss Maisie.

The gentle face. The people she'd helped.

The people she'd killed.

She'd taken "no one's perfect" to the extreme. But it was sobering to realize that there were all shades of white and gray and black in everyone. Sarah had been mean—mostly to her parents, which was sobering to realize now. The trick, she decided, was managing your own shades and trying not to get too crazy so that you started deciding who deserved to live and who deserved to die. The event or events that had sent her down this path—if Vlad or one of his brothers had injured Cal? She'd have picked up a gun and shot him herself.

She couldn't hate Miss Maisie, any more than she could hate Cal for shooting good old Vlad. He'd probably saved her life, or saved her from something pretty nasty, and at what cost to himself? He'd known about PTSD because he had experienced it, she guessed.

I love you.

And she loved him. She could admit it to herself now. He wasn't perfect, though he'd looked pretty heroic and dang near perfect last night. But he was just a man trying to do the best he could in a world that didn't make sense sometimes. A man who needed love, too. Both of their lives were a mix of failures, successes and lots of just getting by. Love wouldn't solve their problems, but it did help make the rough spots less rough from what she'd seen.

She wished she could stay here and he'd come to her —she pulled out her phone and sent him a text hoping he was in the kitchen, too. If he wasn't—

The door to the kitchen creaked and she heard footsteps coming down the hall toward the stairs. Toward her.

Pretty much all of her tensed as she waited…

Cal came into view and looked up at her.

He'd left off the gear, of course, but a hero was a hero, even in blue jeans and a tee shirt. She realized she was smiling as she took in the light in his eyes, the smile lines around those eyes and his mouth. His long, strong body that might be hers for the taking if she could just get the words past the lump in her throat.

He started up. "Not ready to face my family?" he asked—humor, but also worry in his voice.

"Not while they think I'm the other woman to three of you," Sarah managed.

"Ben and Frank sorted that out."

"They confessed?" She sat up straighter.

"Well, they confessed neither of them was dating you."

She rose, but still gripped the banister with one hand. "Progress of a sort."

"For them." His advance toward her was slow, but steady. "It's opened up all sorts of speculation about us."

He stopped on the stair below hers, their gazes level with each other.

"Oh." She needed to be brave, as brave as he'd been. He deserved her courage. She lifted her free hand and placed it against a cheek that was rough, but not too rough, the contact sending a tremble up and down her body. She fought back the urge to stall and gathered all she had into the words, "I love you, too."

There were rewards for bravery, she realized, as the light in his eyes grew so bright she felt tears sting the corners of her eyes. He didn't smile and her own faded. It felt too much for mere smiles.

"I want you to know that this is different," he said, as if he'd been practicing the words, "not because I didn't love my ex-wife. I hate it when people say they never loved someone just because they screwed up and let it die. We both did that. We forgot what we felt and then it was too late. But you're not her, so of course it's different and I won't screw it up. I'll pay attention. My job—"

He stopped and Sarah sensed this was at the heart of their "screwup."

"It's dangerous but it is who I am."

Sarah slid her hand down to his shoulder and brought the other hand into play, too, stroking his shoulders and upper arms, though careful not to stray down to skin. That might just send her up in flames.

"I know." She held his gaze as she tried to pick her words now. "I can't promise not to worry about you and if anything happened to you..." her voice broke for a moment but she made herself continue, "it would break my heart."

He started to speak, but she put her hand over his mouth.

"But I'd rather risk the heartbreak than miss the life we can have together. I'd rather have you in my life for as long as we get, than live without you. A day at a time?"

He yanked her close, burying his head in her shoulder.

His grip was so tight, yet somehow gentle. She hung on as fiercely as she could.

His voice was muffled but as determined as his hold. "Let's get married. As soon as we can."

"Okay." For just a minute she saw what her parents had hoped—her walking down this staircase and taking her dad's arm—but then the past faded. The guy waiting wouldn't have been Cal. "About this house…"

His head lifted and his grin was crooked. "It's your business, and Alex seems to have survived living here okay."

"They'll start calling it the honeymoon house." She matched his grin and raised the ante. "How soon is soon?"

"Today? Tomorrow?"

"We have to wait seventy-two hours in this state," she pointed out.

"Seventy-two hours then," Cal said. He hesitated. "That doesn't leave you much time—"

"I'm sure I can cook up something fun in seventy-two hours," she assured him, "especially with the right encouragement." She angled his head, hoping he'd take the clue.

Of course he took the clue—and her lips—with enthusiasm. He was a cop after all.

THANK you for reading *Fais Do Do Die!* I hope you enjoyed it. While you're waiting for the next book, I hope you'll check out some of my backlist books. :-)

To find out about all my releases, be sure to sign up for my New Release eZine and get a free eBook by visiting my website.

If you enjoyed this book, I hope you'll consider leaving a review. It's not just because I'm needy (even though I try not to be!). Reviews help other readers decide which books to buy. :-)

Also by Pauline Baird Jones

Available in print, digital and audio.

Romantic Suspense

The Big Uneasy Series:

Relatively Risky (1)

Family Treed (A Big Uneasy Short Story)

Dead Spaces (2.0)

Louisiana Lagniappe (3.0)

Worry Beads (4.0)

Fais Do Do Die (5.0)

The Big Uneasy Bundle

Lonesome Lawmen Series:

The Last Enemy

Byte Me

Missing You

Lonesome Mama (Bonus short story)

(The *Lonesome Lawmen* is also available as a digital bundle)

Do Wah Diddy Die

The Spy Who Kissed Me

*Perilously Fun Fiction Bundle (*includes *The Spy Who Kissed Me* and *Do Wah Diddy Die.* Bonus: *Do Wah Diddy Delete Short Story Collection)*

Dangerous Dance

A Dangerous Duet - 2020

Science Fiction Romance/Paranormal

Project Universe Series:

The Key (book 1)

Girl Gone Nova (book 2)

Tangled in Time (book 3)

Steamrolled (book 4)

Kicking Ashe (book 5)

Found Girl (book 6)

Lost Valyr (book 7)

Maestra Rising (book 8)

Project Enterprise: The Short Stories

Time Trap: A Project Enterprise Series Short Story

The Real Dragon

Operation Ark: A Project Enterprise Story

Nebula Nine (time travel adventure)

Open With Care (Christmas collection that includes, "Riding For Christmas" and "Up on the House Top"

Specters in the Storm: A paranormal/steampunk/science fiction romance novella

Out of Time (World War II Time Travel Romance)

Just in Time (An Out of Time Adventure)

An Uneasy Future

(A science fiction romance mystery series set in future New Orleans)

Core Punch (1.0)

Sucker Punch (2.0)

One Two Punch: An Uneasy Future Bundle

Short Story Collections

Project Enterprise: The Short Stories

Do Wah Diddy Delete

Let's Fall in Love

The Real Dragon and other short stories

About the Author

Award-winning, *USA Today* best-selling author Pauline never liked reality, so she writes books. She likes to wander among the genres, rampaging like Godzilla, because she does love peril mixed in with her romance.

To find out more about Pauline or her books:
http://paulinebjones.com